DISCOVERING LOVE

When Kim, accounts manager for an archaeological excavation, meets Alex, the dig manager, a mutual attraction flourishes between them. But Alex's colleague Gloria is not so keen on Kim — might she have her eye on Alex for herself? Meanwhile, Kim's sister Julie — a brilliant mathematician, who flits from one boyfriend to another — appears to be falling in love with David, the rich sponsor of the dig. Is it a harmless flirtation, or will she end up with a broken heart?

SPECIAL MESSAGE TO READERS

THE ULVERSCROFT FOUNDATION
(registered UK charity number 264873)
was established in 1972 to provide funds for
research, diagnosis and treatment of eye diseases.
Examples of major projects funded by
the Ulverscroft Foundation are:-

- The Children's Eye Unit at Moorfields Eye Hospital, London
- The Ulverscroft Children's Eye Unit at Great Ormond Street Hospital for Sick Children
- Funding research into eye diseases and treatment at the Department of Ophthalmology, University of Leicester
- The Ulverscroft Vision Research Group, Institute of Child Health
- Twin operating theatres at the Western Ophthalmic Hospital, London
- The Chair of Ophthalmology at the Royal Australian College of Ophthalmologists

You can help further the work of the Foundation
by making a donation or leaving a legacy.
Every contribution is gratefully received. If you
would like to help support the Foundation or
require further information, please contact:

THE ULVERSCROFT FOUNDATION
The Green, Bradgate Road, Anstey
Leicester LE7 7FU, England
Tel: (0116) 236 4325

website: www.foundation.ulverscroft.com

WENDY KREMER

DISCOVERING LOVE

Complete and Unabridged

LINFORD
Leicester

First published in Great Britain in 2016

First Linford Edition
published 2017

A catalogue record for this book is available
from the British Library.

ISBN 978–1–4448–3437–6

Published by
F. A. Thorpe (Publishing)
Anstey, Leicestershire

Set by Words & Graphics Ltd.
Anstey, Leicestershire
Printed and bound in Great Britain by
T. J. International Ltd., Padstow, Cornwall

This book is printed on acid-free paper

1

Kim looked at him and hoped she sounded more competent than she felt. 'Mr Harrison, there is no reason to raise your voice. I understand completely.'

Alex Harrison ran his hand over his face and pulled himself together.

Kim had researched the various people taking part in the excavation when she got the job. One of the first she had checked was the director, an expert on Roman and Etruscan history. He was standing in front of her, and at the moment he was glowering at her. She decided he wasn't handsome in the classical sense, but he was definitely eye-catching, and there was something about him that told you he was a cut above average. He was in his thirties and nearing six feet tall. He had thick, dark hair, sprinkled with grey at the temples. It was neatly-cut, but she could tell it needed regular attention otherwise it would grow wild. It was too thick and wiry to behave submissively. His eyes were bright blue and were his most appealing feature. They indicated his mood, and at the moment it was stormy. He didn't dress like an academic. At present, he was wearing khaki chinos, a casual shirt, and a leather biker jacket. Kim reasoned that someone who was running an archaeological dig didn't need a city business suit, but she'd expected someone much steadier and more solemn. She concentrated her thoughts on why he was looking so exasperated.

Her defensive amber eyes met his blue appraising ones. She cleared her throat. 'I sympathize, and I understand it's very frustrating, but I can't do anything about the situation at present. As soon as the promised financial backing is transferred to the appropriate account, I'll let you know, and transfer some of it to the site account on the double. Until then, I can't conjure money out of thin air. I have none, so I can't give you any.'

He shoved his hands deep into his pockets. Somehow the movement only emphasised his frustration. 'Do you realize that at present I haven't even any cash to buy a jar of instant coffee to use at the meetings we're having about scheduling the dig?'

Kim shrugged and managed a stiff smile. 'I'm sorry, but the hitches are not my fault, and I can't give you what I don't have. I will talk to Mr Booth when he comes in later this afternoon, and I'll ask him to try to speed up the process in some way. As you know, the excavation is officially sponsored by David Holland, and we have no say in how much money he transfers, or how fast. People like him, from the business world, don't understand the difficulties in getting an excavation going when the money isn't available as promised. They just work with figures and accounts, and aren't concerned with practical difficulties. As far as I understand, Mr Booth, no one is even completely certain how much Mr Holland *is* prepared to finally shell out.' Alex nodded his agreement, and she felt easier with her flow of words. 'I only know that he has agreed to finance the initial survey, and that any additional funds will depend on if you find anything or not and what the future prospects are. In effect, the financial side of things is completely at David Holland's mercy.' His expression was still sceptical, so she just carried on. 'I'm just here to help with the financial organization — that's if, and when, I get some financing to handle! I do the bookkeeping, and act as a kind of go-between between you and Mr Holland. I've never seen Mr Holland, or any of his advisors, and I'm definitely not important enough to be able to put pressure on him in any way. You'll have to wait, I'm afraid.'

His eyebrows rose inquiringly. 'Do

you at least understand anything about archaeology?'

She shoved some errant waves off her face and replied with quiet obstinacy, 'Next to nothing; probably not more than any normal person.'

His expression revealed all, and he said dryly, 'That's great! Just great! I have to liaise with someone who doesn't understand the first thing about running an excavation. I hope you don't expect me to explain archaeological terms every time I give you something to charge to the account? That's when, and if, this account ever transpires.'

Feeling a growing annoyance at his high-handed attitude, she coloured and remained sitting, her slender fingers intertwined tensely in her lap. Despite his frustration, and her own disapproval of his response, there was a vitality and efficiency about him that drew her like a magnet. He interested her very much. She told herself it had something to do with his name and his reputation. 'I've made a glossary of general terms I can refer to when you mention something connected with the excavation, and I've tried to read up on similar projects — what's involved and what happens.'

He gazed at her with a bland half-smile. 'Really? And I suppose you now think you know all about it? It makes me wonder why my students bother to go to university for a couple of years. It looks like they can pick up all they need from the Internet or books.'

He was an attractive man to look at, but she wondered if he was capable of making any friendly conversation. She remained silent for a fraction of a second, then her eyes flashed. 'I don't pretend to be other than marginally informed about what you do, Mr Harrison. I simply want to make things easier for myself by understanding roughly what goes on. I don't need to be an archaeological expert to do the bookkeeping and maintain a methodical account of how you spend the money. In turn, I don't expect you to understand how double bookkeeping works, how to cope with accounting terms, or exactly how to coordinate everything with Mr Holland's accounts department. My job is to keep track of the money. The situation would be completely different if you had funding from the university. Mr Holland wants detailed accounts of how this money is spent — something which, in my opinion, is completely understandable. The only reason I read up on archaeological terms was because I thought I'd then be able to understand, without too much difficulty, anything you mentioned when I needed to enter it in my records — what it is, and what it's for! I wanted to avoid asking questions all the time if I didn't understand some specified item or process.'

Taken aback by the growing antagonism in her tone, and noticing how her chin was stiffening, he stuck his hands in his chinos and considered her more carefully for a moment. She had brown eyes, shot through with tiny fragments of amber near the pupils. They reminded him of pieces of the semiprecious stone he'd found while just walking along the edge of the Baltic Sea not so long ago. She had good bone structure, an oval face, and chestnut hair. She was also definitely full of confidence and poise. He decided it was time to bury his vexation. She was right; it wasn't her fault. As casually as he could manage, he cleared his throat.

'Right! And I suppose there's no point in me trying to talk to Mr Booth at present?'

She was still irked, but remained polite. She shook her head. 'No. Even if he could see you, he wouldn't give you a different answer — unless, of course, he's heard something since I last spoke to him. You can't see him now anyway. He's chairing a meeting and it's likely to last till lunchtime.' She decided that, even if Mr Harrison acted like an bull in a china shop, there was no reason she should be uncivil too. She'd have to get used to his attitude. They'd be working together as long as the excavation lasted. Perhaps he was throwing his weight around because he was a professor and she was an office dogsbody, and he wanted to remind her of the fact. She got up. With slightly heightened colour, she asked, 'I presume he has your telephone number, Mr Harrison?'

She came towards him and he found that she barely reached his shoulder. He wished now he hadn't been hostile and put her back up. Her explanations had disconcerted him. Of course he knew, before he even came through the door, that any delay wouldn't be her fault. She, and he, were mere cogs in the machinery. When she knew him better, she'd appreciate why he was in the habit of trying to control things, and how that meant he was too abrupt and sometimes too curt with others. Perhaps if he hadn't faced the delivery of some incorrect supplies at the site this morning, he wouldn't have been in such a foul mood, and he wouldn't have confronted her so heatedly. Watching her now, he felt sorry that he had. She was clearly intelligent and she had spirit. 'Yes, but I'll leave another one in case he's lost it.' He reached into an inner pocket and handed her his card.

Kim took care that their fingers didn't meet when she took it. 'I'll tell him you called, and that you are waiting for definite information about the financing.'

She had extraordinary eyes. Almond in shape, and the mixture of brown and amber was very unusual. He'd always loved brown eyes. 'Thank you!' He thought a small clarification, a mild admission that she wasn't to blame, wouldn't go amiss. 'I'm just very anxious to get going. Now that we do definitely have a sponsor and we know that the dig can actually take place, it's very frustrating to wait until we're certain the money is there. I don't intend to put my professionals to work unless I'm sure I can pay them. Everyone is raring to go: it's been at the planning stage for far too long.'

She nodded wordlessly and looked composed. He started to turn away.

'Mr Harrison!' He turned back. Kim reached for a jar of instant coffee from the top of a nearby filing cabinet. 'I really do understand. Perhaps this will fill the gap until you have some money to buy your own?' She put it down on the desk in front of him.

Some of the tension in the room faded as his mouth curved into a smile. It was replaced by a grin that overtook his features, and as he picked up the jar his expression took ten years off his appearance. He noted she was wearing washed-out jeans and a checked shirt. Her sandals were sensibly flat and looked comfortable. She hadn't plastered herself with make-up, either. All things considered, she was quite pretty; and studying her closely now, he didn't understand why he'd been so antagonistic. He lifted the jar above his head, jiggled it in the air, and laughed softly before he went towards the door.

2

Mr Booth was a fussy academic. When Kim told him Alex Harrison had called about the sponsored money, his brow furrowed and he commented, 'Oh, dear! That's typical of Alex. He's impatient to get going, but has no idea how difficult it is to persuade outsiders to part with their money. It took the devil's own persuasion to coax David Holland to support the excavation. There's no point in us jumping on Holland's toes at this stage. He might get annoyed and change his mind.'

Kim happened to know that Derek, Mr Booth's assistant, had done all the persuading and negotiating. Mr Booth had only appeared on the scene when things were almost wrapped up. She queried, 'But he does intend to finance the dig?'

'Oh yes! At present, anyway. Derek

has some kind of signed agreement. Perhaps Derek could try to gently nudge the people he deals with. I expect it's always the same with big concerns. The ones at the top decide, but the minions down below have to figure out how to turn the wheels.'

'I read an article about David Holland the other day. He's immensely rich, isn't he? It mentioned he owns an airline, a chain of grocery stores, hotels, online trading, and he's into urban property development. He even owns his own island in the Caribbean.'

'Yes, he's very impressive, and still only in his late thirties. He started off with some financial backing from his father, Lord Holland, but he then went from strength to strength under his own steam.'

'Will you phone Alex Harrison? I said you would.'

'I'll get Derek on to finding out how things stand first, and then phone him. 'He looked around her silent office with its sparse furniture and run-of-the-mill appearance. 'It's probably a bit boring for you at the moment. But that will change. Alex and I will have to talk things through in detail as soon as I hear definitely about the financial position.'

'He's not happy about the delay.'

Mr Booth nodded. 'I can imagine. It must be annoying to know it's been approved but he can't start. Can't be helped! How's your uncle?'

'He's still busy; working on his report about his last contract in New Mexico.'

'Jack always was an excellent geologist. He was one of the best students of his year. His reputation has grown stronger with the passing of time, and with every completed commission.' Mr Booth looked dreamily out of the long window into the garden. Some thin branches of dense greenery outside the windows were slapping the glass in the gusty winds. 'If I hadn't got clogged down by a university administration job after we finished our degrees, and ended up on the management side of things, I might have had a similar kind of career.'

Kim didn't comment, although she thought that if Arnold Booth had really wanted the worries of self-employment after university, he could have gone for it. He'd decided to opt for the safe and secure choice of a working life behind a desk instead. He'd never left university. He'd trod his measured way to become the head of his department instead of becoming a geologist working in the field. Kim reminded herself not to censure him. If Uncle Jack and he hadn't been fellow students, and if Arnold Booth hadn't mentioned they were looking for part-time help when they met up for a drink recently, she wouldn't be here today. It happened at an apt moment. Her previous boss had retired, and as he couldn't find a new associate to take over his solicitor's practice in their small village, he'd had to close it down and she was out of a job.

A couple of days later, Kim sat on the

side, her legs tucked neatly under her chair. She wore a navy pencil skirt and a gold blouse that complimented her colouring. She listened to the conversation between Derek, Mr Booth and Alex Harrison.

Alex leaned back in his chair as it complained about his weight. 'So the financial side has definitely been settled?'

Derek nodded and Arnold Booth hastened to cut in. 'Yes. It's all resolved and organized. The first instalment has already been transferred, and we've opened a new account. Kim has the details and she'll give you a copy. You are free to utilize it as best you can. I know you are always careful to watch where it goes, so I don't need to remind you of that. Holland's people promise two similar payments later — if Holland knows the dig is making progress and he's sure his money is being used wisely.'

'His first instalment won't cover more than the first couple of sections.

Archaeological digs run away with money. If we didn't always have a bunch of enthusiastic volunteers to help onsite, it wouldn't be possible.'

Mr Booth nodded. 'Agreed! And we all know even this funding is pretty basic, but you'll have to do the best you can, I'm afraid. I don't think we can squeeze any more out of them. Holland is not getting any kind of business return on his money, he's just being benevolent.'

Derek nodded.

Alex began to think their talk was a waste of time. His financial framework was a minimum; anyone could tell that. 'What kind of proof does he need to keep the money flowing?'

'Ah! That's where the businessman Holland comes on the scene. He wants a detailed breakdown of your expenditures. He'll only authorize the next payment if he's satisfied with the way the previous sum was spent.'

Alex ran his hand through his hair. 'How ridiculous! Does he expect me to run around the site with a notebook hung around my neck to note down every penny we use? I haven't got time for that kind of thing. I have an excavation to organize and run.'

'No. That's where Kim comes in. It's her job to keep an eye on things, and to arrange and formulate your expenditure in such a way that Holland can see at a glance on paper what's happened to his money.'

A shadow of annoyance crossed Alex's face, and he glanced at Kim. 'In other words, we have a regulator watching us.'

She met his glance. 'If you want to call me that, go ahead. I have no idea what happens on other archaeological excavations, but Mr Holland is clearly someone who watches where his money goes. You can't blame him for that. Handing it over in instalments may be annoying, but if that's what he wants to do, you'll have to knuckle under or do without.' She continued, with a distinct hardening of his eyes, 'I need a comprehensive record of what you do with the money. I'll put it into a decent form for Mr Holland. I also think it wouldn't be a bad idea to give him some kind of rough idea of how you are going to use any future funds. I expect he'll be pleased if he sees that you have financial strategies and you don't plan to use it all up in the first five days.'

He stiffened. 'I am not an incompetent beginner. I know how to handle funding. This isn't the first time I've managed a site excavation.'

She said emphatically, 'I'm sure you do your job wonderfully, but Mr Holland wants details, and I don't think you've had to handle this kind of sponsor before. I am here to help you, Mr Harrison. I am not here to clench my fists tight around the money to stop you from using it. I hope that, in the long run, I may even save you work. You can dictate whatever you authorize instead of making written notes. I'll take it from there and produce decent expenditure reports for him. I can organize the payment of the bills from the fund if you like, or you can go on doing it yourself.' Her throat was dry, but she ploughed on. 'I can imagine that making written notes would be tiresome, that's why I suggest using a Dictaphone. It won't take up much room in your pocket.'

Arnold Booth concurred and added, 'It's a sensible option. We all know how busy you are, once things get going. If you have to make detailed reports to David Holland about expenses, it will be an extra task that you'll hate. But, if you use a Dictaphone, Kim can turn out lists and financial reports in a decent form to present to Holland. If he gets dissatisfied, there's a danger he'll put a lid on supplying any more money.'

'And Miss — ?' Alex glanced across at her.

Derek supplied the missing information. 'Goddard, Kim Goddard.'

'Does Miss Goddard come for free?

Isn't she an extra drain on our tight budget?'

Derek hurried to explain. 'I've managed to get her funded from an extra cash subsidy from one of our foundations. Her earnings are marginal anyway, so she's definitely not a drain on your fund.'

Looking suitably reproached, he glanced at her briefly, and then nodded. 'Okay! So, officially we can get going?'

Arnold nodded. 'We are all eager to find out if your assumptions about the site are accurate, and what you'll find there.'

Alex got up. 'Thank the Lord for that. There's a lot of work to do before the first trowel of earth is moved. We'll turn up something worth finding, I'm sure of that. I wouldn't want to be in charge if I wasn't quite certain. I'll start to spread the word and get my team together.'

'Do that. And keep us informed.'

The meeting broke up and they went their various ways. Kim was surprised to find Alex followed her back to her office.

'It looks like we are stuck with each other.'

She kept her expression neutral. 'So it seems.'

'Do you have a Dictaphone?'

She searched through the things in the desk drawers and said, 'I can't help the situation any more than you can, Mr Harrison. I imagine people like David Holland reach the stage where they have more money than sense, and for some reason your proposed excavation interests him. You should be glad that he's prepared to give you his money. I expect a lot of charity concerns beg for his attention.' She handed him a slightly battered machine. 'That is mine, but it works. It's easy to use, but don't confuse the fast-forward button with the erase button. Try it out first. Surely it's easier talking into that, as things progress, than writing everything down? You can tell me that you've spent ten pounds on some trowels, five pounds on kneeling pads, and one pound fifty for instant coffee, just by pressing a button. I then have a record of how much is spent, and what for, so I can enter it into my accounts.'

He stared. 'You've thought about it seriously, haven't you? How to keep track of everything? Okay, I capitulate!' He smiled at her.

She liked his changed attitude. 'I'm not anti-dig, if you're thinking that I am. I could be someone who doesn't want to see one inch of Gough's Burrow excavated, but I'm not. I *am* interested in what could be there. I read that you do your best to refill a site properly afterwards, that's what encouraged me to accept this job — that, and the fact I'd just lost my other one. Is that all, or can I help in some other way?'

His blue eyes were thoughtful, and suddenly very serious. 'No, I think I have everything I need for the moment. I can even afford my own coffee now.'

Alex watched her as she gave him the desired smile.

She heard him say 'Thanks, Kim!' as he exited. She plonked down gratefully onto the nearest chair and caught her breath.

3

Kim studied the passing scenery as the bus wound its sluggish way home. Uncle Jack owned an old Jeep and Kim had a driving licence, but the bus was cheaper. Staring out of the misted window where someone had drawn a smiley with its tongue sticking out, half of her thoughts were busy with what they'd have for supper, while the other half recalled her meeting with Alex Harrison. He'd been her only visitor all day, and she was still surprised how well she could recall his features.

Ever since her parents died in a car accident, Kim and her sister had lived with Uncle Jack. A lot of the time, he'd been off on some project or other in an outlandish part of the world. He was often forced to leave them to their own devices, because he had no other choice. Someone had to earn money to keep them. He'd left them in the care of his housekeeper, Linda. When they were growing up, he was always either going somewhere or coming back. In the course of time, his erratic lifestyle had made him slightly scatter-brained and forgetful; but Kim and her sister Julie loved him to bits. His unpredictable style of existence suited the two growing girls perfectly. Linda provided them with the stability children needed, and when he was home, he showered them with lots of care and attention.

Although Kim was three years older, it was a foregone conclusion that Julie should be the first to go to university. She was brilliant in school, especially in mathematics and the sciences. The sale of their parents' house had been invested, and that was now providing the backbone for Julie to study without any financial pressures. When Julie finished her degree, if there was still money left over, Kim hoped to study too. Julie had protested at first, but finally agreed, and promised to get through her studies in record time. Kim was filling in the intermittent time with office work, and she also kept an eye on their uncle, the cottage, and all their expenses. Linda had left them for a well-earned retirement. Rheumatism had driven her to it, although she still kept an eye on Jack and the girls. Kim kept an eye on Uncle Jack, and battled hard to make Julie understand she couldn't afford to join in each and every pastime mentioned on the university noticeboard.

Today, Julie was home on a flying visit, and while they ate a vegetarian lasagne that evening, Kim told them about Alex Harrison. Uncle Jack disappeared into his study after the meal. Julie was her usual curious self, and she began to search the Internet for information about the man.

When she found what she was looking for, she exclaimed, 'Lord! The way you described him, I thought he'd look like a superstar! He's positively ancient!'

Kim laughed. 'No, he's not. You think anyone over the age of twenty-five is ancient.' She tried to peer over Julie's arm. 'Does it say how old he is?'

Julie read his date of birth and calculated. 'He's thirty-three!'

'That's not old, love, and apparently he's very famous in his field of archaeology.'

'Hmm! So it seems,' she admitted reluctantly. 'He's not bad-looking, and an associate professor already . . . but if he's anything like Uncle Jack, he'll be a nightmare on two legs.' She looked up at her sister with beautiful turquoise eyes. Her honey-coloured ponytail bounced around as she did so.

Kim chuckled. 'Oh, somehow I don't think he's like Uncle Jack. Uncle Jack has always lived in a world of his own, hasn't he? He's so disorganized, I sometimes wonder why he has such a terrific reputation — but perhaps he does his work in a very systematic way, better than we imagine. I had the opposite impression when I met Alex

Harrison. He doesn't beat about the bush, he seems very well-organized, and he thinks in a practical and logical way. I imagine he's on top of his job.'

'Aha! Are you showing some interest in a man at last?'

Kim shook her head. 'Don't be silly! I've only seen him once or twice, and he didn't take the slightest notice of me in that way. We are not all like you. You collect and discard your boyfriends like there's no tomorrow.'

'Well, it's better to do that than to ignore the possibilities. Everyone falls in and out of love all the time these days.'

'Do they? Then it isn't real love, it's probably more like a chemical reaction. Remember that quantity doesn't necessarily always mean quality.'

Julie tossed her head and her eyes sparkled. 'But it's fun! You don't get enough fun. Don't tell me that boring Nigel Parker makes your heart flutter with excitement. He's about as exhilarating as a bag of soggy chips.'

'Nigel is okay. He's a friend, a good

friend. We've known him all our lives.'

Julie tilted her head to the side. 'Well make sure you don't end up with him, or I'll refuse to visit you. You should have gone to university first, Kim. It would have given you a couple of years of freedom, and a new perspective.'

Kim laughed. 'You know only one of us can go at a time. You were always super-brainy. It was obvious that you had to go straight from school. If you'd hung around waiting for me, it would have been a real shame. I don't mind, honest: cross my heart! I'm happy with my life as it is at present.'

'When I'm qualified, I swear I'll finance you, even if there's not enough in the kitty — whatever you want to do. You need proper qualifications these days . . . And stop doing yourself down all the time! You got excellent A-levels, and you are just as intelligent. It's only a quirk that I have this unusual talent for mathematics.'

'And that must be encouraged and fostered. I bet the others are surprised to have a fellow student who looks like the fairy on the Christmas tree but has a brain like Einstein.'

Julie giggled. 'Yes, it was fun when I first arrived. In fact, it still is — especially when I manage to trip up one of the professors. Don't change the subject! You should be doing something you love, learning something proper.'

'Don't nag! I'm saving my pennies. I might do an Open University course while you're still busy with your degree. So don't worry about me. We'll both make it, even if we use two different routes to reach our goal.'

Julie's brows lifted. 'Really? That's good. What are you thinking of taking?'

Kim shrugged. 'History, perhaps; art combined with something else; or languages. As soon as I have the details and know I can afford it, I'll start to think seriously about what I want to do.' She looked at her watch. 'By the way, it's your turn to do the washing-up.'

Julie scowled. 'Yuck! And I've just

done my nails! You were always good at art. Your drawings were always super. I have a couple on the wall in my room. Several people have commented on how skilled they are. I'm glad you're making plans, though.' Julie frowned. 'Why did you take this job? There must be something else locally that pays more.'

'I think I'm going to like it, and it's only temporary. I do intend to look for something else, but jobs are not thick on the ground at the moment. It suits me fine. My wages keep things ticking over. Uncle Jack covers all the overheads here, so I can use my money as I like. What time are you leaving tomorrow?'

'Straight after breakfast. I don't have a lecture until after lunch, so I don't need to catch the first bus out.'

'Good.' Kim looked forward to a quiet night at home with her sister. While Julie got up to stack the dishes on the draining board, she went into the living room and switched on the TV.

Looking around, she was pleased she'd replaced the winter foliage in the open fireplace yesterday. Willow House was at least three hundred years old. It had blackened beams and low ceilings. The windows had insets with diamond-shaped glass. In the winter, the frames let in draughts; but in summer, they gave the place a very comfortable and romantic atmosphere. Kim loved the house. She couldn't remember much about her parents' home any more.

★   ★   ★

A few days later, Alex Harrison phoned her at the office. When she recognized his deep voice, Kim lost her own words for a moment, but she recovered quickly.

'I have a gap in my timetable this morning. Would it be suitable for me to call?'

'Yes, of course. What for?'

'I'd like us to coordinate the various steps we need to take. It will help me organize my schedules, and perhaps it will help you to have a framework for the different stages of the diverse expenses when they come about.' He sounded quite friendly for a change.

'That sounds like a good idea. I've borrowed a second Dictaphone, so you won't have to hang around waiting for the first one. We could buy extra tapes, but it's just as easy to exchange machines if we have two.'

'Fine. Good idea! I'll be there in about half an hour, then.'

She straightened her skirt, applied some fresh lipstick and combed her hair. He arrived sooner than she'd estimated. She heard his silver BMW come to an audible halt on the gravel driveway outside the building. She peeped through the side window, and she caught him looking at her before he walked towards the door. He gave her the inkling of a smile and she just felt embarrassed.

She registered that she seemed unsettled. Kim associated it with her discussion about him with Julie — all about if he was boyfriend material, or not. Looking at her carefully, he took off his jacket and hung it on the back of a nearby chair.

'Would you like a cup of coffee?'

'If it's no trouble.'

'No, of course not.'

Alex noticed her uneasiness. He was accustomed to analysing the atmosphere in the lecture room, or the expressions of his students and other workers. He realized he'd probably ruffled her feathers the other day, but he was surprised that he cared. Generally he was too single-minded to be bothered about what others thought. He always tried to say what he believed because it cut out any misunderstandings. People knew they could be honest with him too, and say what they wanted, but they had to know him well first. This girl was practically a stranger.

In spite of that, he didn't get the impression she lacked the confidence to be frank with him, because her answers up to now had been direct and to the point. She probably hadn't liked the tone he'd adopted, and he admitted that sometimes it might seem harsh to a newcomer. He ran his hand over his face and waited as she brought him a mug of coffee. He crossed one ankle over his knee and told himself she'd get used to him eventually.

She asked, 'Sugar?'

'No thanks.' He added the extra information: 'You don't always have the luxury of sugar or milk on digs that are far from civilization. I've got used to doing without.'

Her reply was perfectly controlled and polite. 'My uncle is the same.'

He took a sip. 'Your uncle?'

'He's a geologist. Jack Goddard.'

'Really? Jack Goddard's your uncle? I've met him a couple of times at conferences. He did a great analysis in what was formerly Mesopotamia a couple of years ago, and he's cleared the way for a lot of gas and oil discoveries in his time, hasn't he?'

She cupped her mug in her hands. 'Yes, I think so. Uncle Jack doesn't talk much about his work when he's at home. We probably wouldn't understand what he's going on about, anyway.'

'We?' His curiosity was wakened.

'My sister and I. We live with him.'

'Oh, I see.' She didn't offer any more information, and Alex decided not to probe. He put his mug on the desk, and leaned back in the chair. Searching the pockets of his loose jacket, he found the recorder and positioned it next to the mug. 'I've noted everything I think we should aim for when breaking down expense records. See what you think.' He viewed her carefully when he added, 'Perhaps it is just as well you will get a vocal record of what I use the money for. I'm told that my writing looks like a drunken spider gone haywire!'

She managed a slight smile. 'If that's true, then the Dictaphone will save us both work. Otherwise, I might drive you mad for explanations and translations.

Uncle Jack has appalling handwriting, but I'm used to his by now.' She hastened to explain, 'I type his final reports.'

'You seem to be busy. Working here. Working for your uncle.'

'It's not demanding. I'm helping him, not working for him, and he's only home between commissions. He doesn't need me to organize *all* his paperwork.' She picked up his recorder. 'I'll sort out what's on this, and perhaps next time you come in, I can agree or disagree; just in case we differ about an idea?' She felt it was only polite to ask. 'How are the preparations going?'

'Fine. Derek mentioned that David Holland intends to come and look at the site one day soon. It seems strange that he's so interested, especially when you know he's never had anything to do with digs and archaeology before.'

Tongue in cheek, she said, 'Perhaps he was fascinated when he was a boy, but wasn't allowed to get too interested. Some parents probably don't see a rosy financial future for an archaeologist. He comes from a very wealthy and traditional background, doesn't he? They probably didn't want him messing about in the mud for the rest of his life.'

He smiled broadly, and Kim caught her breath when she felt the effect. 'You're right there. Our profession definitely doesn't shower us with financial accolades.'

'But you travel the world, and you're working in your chosen career. That's what my uncle tells me is his consolation whenever I ask why he chose to become a geologist. Who knows how many high-flyers in the financial world are really satisfied with the lives they lead?'

He stood up. 'Maybe you're right, but not all archaeologists travel the world. A lot of us end up in the permanent employment of universities, museums, foundations and such, because at some stage in our lives we need financial security. Most of us don't go on digs beyond the UK, but I agree that our work gives nearly all of us great satisfaction. I think it may be even more difficult for a geologist to be independent. Most of them work for international companies who are merely looking for new sources of oil, gas, minerals, or other kinds of natural resources and deposits. Your uncle has managed to remain independent only because he's so good. Companies want to employ him because they get exact reports.'

'The same applies to you, doesn't it? You can now pick and choose because of your reputation.' His brows lifted and he studied her for a moment. She ploughed on. 'Well, that's what I gather from listening to other people.'

A soft smile emerged and the corners of his mouth turned up. 'Could be! I hope so. I try to give one hundred percent and more, every time.'

She ruffled some papers on her desk and nodded. She opened the drawer and handed him a second recorder. 'You'll need this now, and perhaps you

40

can start to record all expenses immediately?'

He picked it up and considered it. 'Where do you get all these? Do you have shares in the factory?'

He had successfully disarmed her, and they shared a smile. 'The first one is mine, that one is a spare. Uncle Jack takes it with him when he's out in the field. He's at home at the moment, so it's just lying around.'

He drained his mug and put it down. He got up and lifted the new recorder. 'Thanks for this. I'll do my best to cover everything.'

Kim nodded. 'Till next time, then? If I can do anything to help, just let me know. I'm useless as far as the dig is concerned, but I'm good at organizing and at finding suppliers, items needed, or anything along those lines.'

He turned and headed for the door. 'Will do! Bye, Kim!' He turned back. 'Do you think I could have a word with him some time — with your uncle? I'd like to meet him again. I'd value his geological knowledge about the site. It isn't often I have the chance to talk with an expert who knows the area like the back of his hand, and about the ground structure.'

She met his glance. 'Yes, of course. I'm sure he'd like to see you if you've met him before.' She scribbled their telephone number and their address on a pad, and ripped the page off. 'Phone him and explain.'

He took it. 'I will. Thanks again!' Somehow, he felt better that they were parting on more pleasant terms this time.

With something close to regret, she watched him go, and even looked out of the window until his car disappeared from sight.

4

A few days later, Alex did phone Uncle Jack, and the two men agreed to meet at the weekend.

Her uncle was surprisingly accommodating when Saturday morning arrived. He'd even changed his shirt when he came down to breakfast. His grey hair was receding, and his greenish eyes had a permanent sardonic twinkle that gave him a mischievous air. He always ate sparingly, and this morning was no exception. As usual, a piece of toast and some coffee was all he needed. Even though he usually took his breakfast straight to his study, this morning he sat at the kitchen table with her, and Kim stroked his grey hair discreetly into place as she poured him his coffee. Sunshine struggled past the bunched side-curtains and spread itself across the table. She sat down and buttered her own toast. She enjoyed the luxury of an unhurried breakfast; frequently she ate her toast on the way to the bus stop because she was late.

He looked across at her. 'You're a good girl, Kim. I'm proud of you.'

Surprised by his words, her eyes widened. She couldn't love him more if he was her real father. He was often vague and distracted, but he was a kind, gentle person. 'It's not hard to be good when you're around.'

He sipped his coffee. 'Ah! But I know that I'm often so preoccupied that I sometimes cause unnecessary work . . . but I am grateful for your help and care. You know that, I hope?

She patted his hand. 'Yes, of course. We can never repay what you did for us. I'm glad if I can repay you in some way now and then.'

After breakfast, Kim rushed to tidy the sitting room before Alex was due to arrive. He was punctual. She heard his car stopping outside. His person filled the doorway and cut out the light. An easy smile played at the corner of his mouth, and Kim offered him a smile in return when she answered the door.

He tilted his head to the side. 'Is it still convenient?'

'Yes, come in. Watch your head! The beams are very romantic, but they're a hazard for tall people like yourself.'

He nodded and looked around. 'It's a very nice cottage. It was built when most people were generally shorter. Don't worry! My parents have a similar sort of cottage in the Cotswolds. I grew up learning to be careful!'

'Good! I won't keep warning you, then. Follow me. Uncle Jack is in the sitting room. He's looking forward to seeing you.' She waited until they shook hands, and then left them.

After the door closed behind her, Alex commented, 'Your niece is very nice.'

'She is. Don't know what I'd do without her anymore. Her sister is at university in Leicester. The two of them have lived with me since their parents were killed in a car crash. Kim was ten and Julie seven when it happened.' He indicated to the coffee things Kim had already left on the coffee table. 'Help yourself. Kim always makes coffee in a vacuum jug for me, because she knows I forget that it's there most of the time.'

Alex leaned forward and poured himself a cup. Jack raised his hand to indicate he didn't want any. 'How did you manage to cope with the sudden arrival of two young children in your life? That must have been very difficult for a bachelor. I think you aren't married?'

Jack shook his head. 'My nomadic life didn't leave me much time to find someone who'd put up with it. Luckily, I already had a housekeeper. Linda was very capable, and slipped into the mother role. She lived in and watched over them when I was away. She retired two years ago. Since then, Kim has been handling things, and she does it well. I can concentrate on my work and I know she manages the rest. I'm proud of them both. They are the daughters I never had.'

'And I'm sure they appreciate what you did.'

'I decided I wanted to, and hoped it would work out. It did, much better than I'd imagined.' He cleared his throat. 'Well, tell me about your project. Kim mentioned it's a dig on Gough's Burrow? I think the topsoil is a fine sediment, isn't it?'

Alex nodded and the two men started talking and were soon lost in the technicalities of what was there and what might be expected. Kim kept out of the way and went out into the garden. She busied herself with tidying one of the flowerbeds. She grappled with the weeds and wondered where half of them came from. No one else was interested in the garden, but Kim often found it was a relaxing place to think out plans and solve problems. Perhaps it had something to do with her being on her own and in the fresh air.

Some time later, she heard footsteps behind her on the gravel and turned to face Alex. She felt untidy and her face was warm. There was a faint buzzing of bees plundering a nearby flowering creeper on trelliswork attached to the wall. 'Oh! Are you finished already? Uncle Jack often forgets the time when a colleague comes round.'

'I'd like to stay longer, but I have to interview some volunteers who want to give up their time to help us. Your uncle has promised to come to look at the site one day soon. It would be disastrous to dig up that hill and find nothing . . . but I'm very confident, and your uncle is too!' His expression was full of anticipation.

Clutching her secateurs tightly in gloved hands, she retorted, 'Mr Harrison, I'm sure that you'd never excavate a site unless you were certain there was something there worth finding. You wouldn't be so renowned if you just dug holes all over the place with nothing to show for your efforts.'

He laughed. She liked the sound of it, and secretly admired his long, lean form.

'Perhaps. But there's always a first time, and I could land face-down in the muck . . . but somehow I honestly think it is a spot worth checking. I don't base things on mere hunches and local beliefs. I'm Alex, by the way!'

She nodded. 'Did he mention when he'd like to visit you?'

'No. He told me he's still busy with his report from his last expedition, but I hope it will be soon. We'll see each other again before long, I hope?'

Kim was flustered. 'I expect so.' She paused, but he didn't seem so intimidating any more, so she asked, 'I'd enjoy seeing the site, too — that's if you don't mind me coming with him.'

'No, of course not. Any time! We do try to control visitors, because we can never be sure if someone will unwittingly cause damage.' He paused. 'In your case, I'm sure you realize you need to be careful.' She coloured. 'Oh, by the way, thanks for the coffee. It was excellent.'

She caught her breath. 'You're welcome.'

He turned on his heel and then twisted to add, 'I'll look forward to seeing you on site. Perhaps you can give me a warning? I'd like to be there when you come.'

Kim nodded, and watched him disappear around the corner of the cottage. A minute or two later, his car sprang to life and she heard him as he reversed back into the narrow side-road. The village had one main street and tapering side-lanes leading off it. There were several old cottages like theirs, and a church that dated back to medieval times. She had an urge to go to the gate and follow his progress but told herself not to be ridiculous. She looked up and saw Uncle Jack watching her from his study. She gave him a thumbs-up. He nodded and smiled broadly.

When she got home from work on Monday, she answered the phone and heard a cultivated voice. 'Good afternoon! My name is Gloria Thurston. Mr Jack Goddard talked to my boss about visiting Gough's Burrow one day soon. He asked me to talk to Mr Goddard and arrange a meeting.'

'Sorry, he has a visitor at the moment. Perhaps we can arrange something? I have his appointment diary in front of me now . . . ' Uncle Jack didn't have a visitor. He didn't know the name Thurston. It would take too long to explain. Anyway, she sounded snooty, and Uncle Jack was too wrapped up in his report at present to leave it for a mere telephone call.

Gloria's voice was impatient. 'I suppose so. Alex asked if Thursday afternoon would be convenient. Is that possible?'

'Just a moment, I'll check.' She didn't need to check anything; she just wanted to sound professional. She rustled the pages of the telephone directory. A minute later, she replied, 'That'll be fine. What time?'

'Three o'clock on the dot. Does he know where Gough's Burrow is?'

Trying not to sound irritated, Kim said, 'Yes. We live in the area and we know Gough's Burrow very well.'

'Good, then he won't need directions, will he? Alex appreciates punctuality. He has another meeting later on, so there is not much leeway in his schedule.'

'He'll be there on time. Oh, your boss also mentioned that he wouldn't mind if I came along with my uncle. That's still okay, I hope?'

There was a definite moment of silence. 'If Alex said you can come, then come with him by all means.'

'Thank you for calling, Ms Thurston.'

Without another word, there was a click and they were disconnected. Kim thought it was an odd way to end a telephone call. She hadn't even said goodbye. Perhaps she didn't like visitors full stop. She wondered exactly what Gloria Thurston did on site.

She pushed wisps of hair off her face and considered her plans for the day. The kitchen needed a going-over, and she'd visit Linda later on. She hadn't seen her for several days. Kim knew that Linda called regularly to see her uncle and share an afternoon cup of tea. She was one of the few non-related people that Uncle Jack didn't choose to ignore. She knew their former house-keeper would always have a place in his life and in theirs. She was the replacement for the mother that the two girls didn't remember very well any more.

★ ★ ★

'And what's your new boss like?' Linda picked up a plate and offered Kim a piece of cherry cake.

'He's okay. He's a bit fussy, and he

tends to push the actual work onto his assistant. Derek puts up with it and doesn't seem to mind. Keeping the records for the archaeological dig doesn't keep me busy all the time, so I help Derek or anyone else from the department with typing or whatever they need doing.'

Linda took a sip from her cup. 'I heard that they were planning to dig for treasure on Gough's Burrow. There was even an article about it in the midweek newspaper. I wonder if they'll find something.'

Kim laughed softly. 'I think the excavation director wouldn't appreciate the word *treasure*. He hopes to find items of historical interest. Apparently, the Romans liked to construct their defences on hills and hummocks like Gough's Burrow — it gave them a better chance of defence if the presumptuous locals attacked them for some reason. Probably the Saxons used the same site for the same reason later on. Alex is more interested in Roman relics, because he's a bit of an expert on that era; but if they find anything Saxon, that will be an extra bonus, of course.'

'Have they started yet?'

Kim nodded and swallowed the cake she was chewing. 'They've broken the topsoil on a couple of units. A unit is an area of ten by ten feet. Alex has invited Uncle Jack to take a look around the site, and I'm going with him.'

'Who is Alex? What does he do? Should I know the name?'

'He's the archaeologist in charge. He's very plain-spoken and candid, and I bet he isn't always an easy person to work for, but he gets results; and people who've worked with him shower him with praise in the end.'

'Married?'

'No, I don't think so.'

'How old?'

Kim shrugged. 'Mid-thirties, and he's quite attractive. If he had a gentler approach in the way he handles people, he'd be a very interesting academic.'

'Aha!'

Kim laughed and her eyes twinkled. 'Don't get any wrong ideas. He's not my type at all.'

'Pity! I'm waiting for the day you tell me you've found someone special. Julie has never had any problems gathering men friends, even though I don't approve of the way she leaves them all high and dry. I can't remember you showing more than a passing interest in anyone.'

Kim pushed her hair off her face. 'That's because we function differently. Julie thinks it's okay to play around with someone's feelings; I don't. It's not fair, and I keep telling her so. I don't see the point in trying to wind a man round your little finger if you know that you're not really interested in him.'

Linda laughed. 'You're right, but Julie was always more casual in her approach, and you were always more serious. She doesn't intend to hurt anyone, she just doesn't realize the effect she has on men.'

'It would do her good if someone put a ring through her nose and led *her* around for a change! It might stop her enjoying life at someone else's cost.'

Linda laughed. 'Don't give her ideas — and don't mention rings through her nose! I'd be devastated if she suddenly had her nose pierced. She has such a lovely face. I don't understand why anyone needs this piercing . . . or those tattoos, either. Wait until they're old and wrinkled, they'll look like shrivelled oranges with markings! Are you still going around with Nigel?'

'Yes: we're good friends, nothing more. He feels safe with me, and I hope he knows he's free if he finds a real girlfriend. Neither of us are likely to meet anyone else around here. Most of the people we know are either married, engaged, or have a steady partner. Nigel and I are companions for visits to the cinema and when a partner is otherwise required.'

Linda sighed. 'That's why I wished you'd gone to university too. It would have given you a complete new slant on life. Jack would have muddled on without you for a while. He'd have filled in the time with a few more commissions in some unassailable part of the world.'

Kim reached out and stroked her hand. 'I intend to go there one day, you know that. I'm not unhappy or dissatisfied. It's not hard being at home with Uncle Jack. I know my present job is only a temporary one, and I intend to find something more permanent soon. It's a gap-filler — and, to be honest, it's more interesting than I expected. I'm getting an insight into what's going on at Gough's Burrow.'

Linda looked sceptical.

Kim said. 'David Holland is financing the dig. Have you ever heard of him?'

'Is he? Yes, of course. He's a well-known entrepreneur, and always in the papers these days. There were pictures of him in a magazine I read the other day. He was launching another cargo carrier for his fleet, at some ship-building yard in Korea.'

'Someone mentioned that he's thinking of visiting the site. He's sponsoring the dig. I expect he wants to check that his money is being used sensibly.'

'He comes from an affluent family, and he's turned their average wealth into an unbelievable fortune. If you can believe the newspapers, he's one of the UK's richest men these days. There was an article about the family in one of the magazines I borrow from Susie.' She got up and started to ruffle through a pile of glossy periodicals on a side table. Kim noticed the joints of her hands looked swollen, and she was probably in pain, but Linda never complained.

'Here's it is, with a picture. He's not only rich, he's good-looking too; and, according to the article, he's never short of an attractive partner.'

Kim took the magazine and studied the picture. The man was tall and slim. His blond hair was styled, but the wind was playing havoc with it in this particular picture. He looked directly at the photographer, and even though it was only a picture, Kim decided he was a man in control. The people around him looked mesmerized and nervous, as if his word was law. In a dark business suit he appeared cultivated and at ease with himself. There were some traces of amusement in his expression. He had pale eyes; she presumed they must be either grey or blue.

She handed the magazine back to Linda. 'Yes, he's very good-looking; and if he is rich and powerful, he must be a very interesting man.'

'Perhaps you'll meet him if he comes to visit Gough's Burrow.'

'I shouldn't think so. I expect he'll make a flash visit to the site and then disappear in his private jet again. There's no reason for him to visit the office; it's miles from the actual dig.'

'Stranger things have happened. Perhaps he'll take a shine to you.'

Kim laughed. 'Oh, Linda! You read too many romantic novels. People like

David Holland never mix with people like us. They live in another world. I'd need to be startlingly beautiful, be in the right place, and have very loose morals to stand a chance. As none of those things apply, I'm not a likely quarry. Never mind about that. How are you? How is your rheumatism? Have you seen the doctor recently?'

Linda shrugged. 'You know he can't do more than prescribe painkillers. I try to manage without them. It takes me longer to do my work these days, but I manage, and I get there in the end. I worry about you and Jack sometimes, though, but I know I could never cope with the work at the cottage anymore.'

'You still keep an eye on us, and you are always there when we need a shoulder to cry on. This flat is one of the first places Julie heads for when she comes home. Knowing how empty-headed Julie is about most things, that is a great compliment. I'm sure Jack loves your chats when you call, so please come around as often as you can. I try to keep things spick and span, but I'll never achieve your standards. We miss you, but you are always there for us, and that's terribly important. Keep checking with the doctors — you never know when some new medication will come onto the market that might all the difference.'

Linda patted her hand. 'You're a good girl. I hope I'll be around to see you find someone who is good enough to deserve you.'

5

Kim asked Derek if she could leave early on Thursday. She told him why. Her work was all up to date and there was nothing else that couldn't wait until tomorrow.

Derek gestured towards the door. 'Off you go. I haven't been there myself yet. I'd like to see the site myself, but Alex doesn't encourage visitors. They distract the workers, and someone has to keep an eye on them and what they're doing.'

'I expect my uncle knows how to act. I think Alex intends to show us around, so he won't let us trample around irresponsibly or cause any trouble.'

Derek nodded. 'Enjoy yourself. Don't worry about old Booth, he's attending a conference in Bournemouth. I don't expect to see him again this week unless we hear David Holland is coming. He'll come back like a shot if that happens. Tell me all about what you saw tomorrow.'

'I'll make up the lost time next week. I'll stay an hour longer each day until I've levelled things out.'

He smiled at her. 'Don't worry about it, Kim. You are sometimes too conscientious for your own good. Skiving for a few hours is okay. Other people do it all the time.'

Kim had driven to work in Uncle Jack's old Jeep that morning so that she could get home faster. When she got there, he'd forgotten about the meeting with Alex. Looking wistfully at the pile of papers on his desk, he got up. 'I'll just get my jacket, and we can be off . . . '

Kim was glad that he didn't want to take the wheel. He was used to driving in the wilds, and his skills and concentration weren't always up to scratch. Sometimes he was away from civilization for weeks or months at a time, and needed to adjust to normal conditions when he returned. As soon as he was used to the speed and amount of traffic, everything was fine again, but she often had to remind him there were hundreds of other drivers on the road — and that traffic lights were there for a purpose. She was always afraid that he'd cause an accident one day, but so far that hadn't happened.

She was familiar with the route. As they approached the actual site, metal safety barriers marked the route to a parking area at the foot of the hill. They got out and walked to the dig location, where people were rushing around with materials and equipment. Uncle Jack asked one of them where they could find Alex Harrison, and he pointed in the direction of a prefabricated metal hut. On the way there, they saw various boxes and crates waiting to be transported to nearby tents or stored elsewhere.

Kim knocked on the hut door and they went straight in.

Alex was standing with papers in his

hand. He was explaining something to a slim woman who was dressed in stylish trousers and a floral blouse with long sleeves. A long silver chain with an ancient-looking motif dangled along the front of the shirt-style top, and she wore matching silver earrings. She was blonde and very attractive and almost as tall as Alex. She could easily have been a smartly-dressed city secretary. Kim wondered if it was just her imagination, or whether the woman's expression darkened a little when she saw them approaching.

Alex smiled and met them half-way. His grin had a calming and reassuring effect on Kim, and she immediately forgot about his colleague's less-than-welcoming expression.

'That's good. You're dead on time.' He glanced at them both, but his eyes seemed to linger a little longer on Kim. Was that true, or just her wishful thinking?

He introduced his colleague. 'This is Gloria Thurston. She's my right hand,

and I couldn't manage without her. Her official title is Archaeological Site Assistant.'

Gloria smiled at him, clearly basking in his attention, especially as they were with strangers. Kim told herself not to be childish. She didn't know a thing about the woman. They had only spoken to each other on the phone once, but since then Kim had characterized her as discourteous because of the abrupt ending. She wondered if Gloria was completely obsessed with her job as Alex's assistant — and also with him as a person.

Alex put the papers down on the desk. He looked at their feet briefly. 'That's good — you both have sensible shoes.' Looking at Kim, he continued, 'You'd never believe the number of women who wander round the site in high heels! So, follow me. I'll try to keep my explanations simple. You've seen enough excavations already, Jack; but I think this is all new to Kim, isn't it?'

Sunshine, spilling through the small window behind her back, transformed Kim's hair to burnished copper. Alex decided that she was not merely a very attractive woman. After having spoken to her a couple of times, he also liked her attitude to life in general. He'd developed a feeling for people's strength and weaknesses. Kim was down-to-earth and she had no illusions. She'd shown patience about his demands, and she displayed kindness, patience and dependability in her personal lifestyle. When he compared her to someone like Gloria, who seemed driven purely by a ruthless aim for praise and recognition, she was a very refreshing contrast. Gloria was a first-class academic, but her ambition was eating her alive. He was glad to have her as part of the team because of her experience, and the way she helped to keep pressures off him. He didn't appreciate her perpetual inferences that they were a perfect team, or that they ought to write a book together. Still sillier, she sometimes mentioned that they belonged together permanently. He presumed she meant in a professional way. He wasn't sure if it was only that, but he'd have to make sure she understood he felt no emotional ties to her in any way. He didn't have time for meaningless affairs with his employees. He couldn't remember when he'd last felt deeply about a woman. He liked them, but he wouldn't be surprised if he ended up as a crusty old solitary academic. He wouldn't want anything second-best. It would be great to have a wife and a family if he ever met the right person . . . but he was leaving it up to fate.

He turned to his assistant. 'Coming, Gloria? Or are you too busy?'

Gloria looked at the papers on her desk. Kim hoped that she'd refuse, but she was disappointed. Gloria glanced up and said, 'No, there's nothing that can't wait for an hour. I'll come too.'

Alex led the way and they followed him towards the foot of the slope. He was wearing a light grey hoodie over a red check flannel shirt and khaki chinos. His dark brown leather hiker boots looked well-worn and were probably very comfortable. Uncle Jack sauntered along at his side. Gloria stuck like a limpet to Kim, although she made no attempt to converse with her. Kim decided not to make an effort either. She guessed that for some reason Gloria resented their coming. But Alex had invited them, so there was nothing she could do about it.

They reached the area where helpers were marking out squares with strings and a spirit level. Alex explained, 'We start off with one or two units in an exploratory dig, although we are pretty sure we'll find things. If we do, we'll explore a wider area.'

Kim remarked, 'How do you choose the right spot to start? Local beliefs? Written clues?'

'We study its strategic position carefully. If a place was on the marching routes between Roman military sites, we check written references to it, where the next post was — that sort of thing. Once we can roughly guess where things might be, we mark off units of ten feet by ten, define our so-called string line using a spirit level, and note where north is in relation to the unit on our plans. Romans built their forts more or less to a set pattern, and the Saxons constructed their houses to face the sun in order to have the benefits of warmth and light. I won't bore you with too many technical expressions . . . We go down, level by level, and record and examine as we go along. Much of the area around here was covered with forests in Saxon and Roman times, and fairly flat, so this particular position was always higher than the surrounding countryside. Elevated defences raised the chances of successfully resisting and rebuffing enemy attack. This place was good as a defence position locally, and as a central assembly point.'

Kim commented, 'It must have almost seemed like punishment for a

Roman soldier to be sent to an outpost like this. I presume it was pretty cut-off, if it was surrounded by a forest and far from the next post or settlement. And then, on top of that, they had to put up with the cold, and rainy British weather.'

He laughed. 'True! I bet they were bored to tears most of the time, unless they were kept busy during a time of unrest or whenever the local population was in uproar. The Romans who were stationed here were probably auxiliary troupes recruited from the Balkans, the Low Countries and Spain, under Legionary control. If they came from sunny climes, like you said, they probably hated the weather, and they had to obey strict military regulations. It must have been difficult for their commanding officers to keep them fit and motivated, but small Roman outposts like this one were spread out like pearls on a string, and they enabled the Romans to keep control of a region once it had been conquered.' He gestured to the group of people measuring the ground nearby. Kim saw that one of them was making notes and drawing diagrams 'We dig as deep as we need to go; we record all the details about position et cetera, carefully as we go deeper; and, naturally, we record and save whatever we find on the way, if we find anything.'

'Are they all paid workers?'

'No. Nearly all of them are volunteers. They are either studying archaeology or some related subject, or are merely enthusiastic amateurs. They just get food and, if possible, somewhere to sleep for their help.' Tongue-in-cheek, he added, 'They are sometimes unkindly referred to as 'trowel fodder', but they are the backbone of what goes on, and we wouldn't be able to do excavations without their help.'

She viewed the group. 'So, you start off somewhere, and extend the search when you find something worth uncovering?'

'Yes, or we just manage with spot

excavations if the money doesn't stretch far enough to uncover a whole site.'

'And you cover it all in again afterwards?'

'Yes, most of the time we refill the whole area. You can't hang on to every historical site. Only the really interesting, extensive ones, worth showing to the public, remain open and survive. Sometimes the local authority agrees to take them over and open them for general viewing, but that involves caring for and preserving the site. The number of interested visitors who'll visit them doesn't generally cover the costs involved, so authorities are reluctant to get too involved even if it is a site of great interest.'

'Will this be an extensive dig?'

He shrugged and gestured with his hands. His fingers were long and tapered; the palms square and workmanlike 'That depends on *if* we find something, when we find it, what we find, and how fast. It's sometimes like looking for a needle in a haystack.

There may be very interesting finds underground, but if you choose the wrong spot when you start, you may hit zero, and then it's hard to convince anyone to invest more time and money. We're under more pressure here, because our sponsor is a private individual who wants to see some kind of rapid return on his outlay.'

Kim stuck her hands in her anorak and let the cool breeze untidy her hair. She felt very comfortable with him. 'Have you ever met David Holland?'

'Yes, briefly, a couple of times. He was very interested and he told me he'd watched a team of archaeologists unearthing a Roman fort near where he comes from when he was growing up. It must have left a strong impression on him. When the university put out feelers for sponsors for this dig, he eventually showed interest. He's a businessman down to his handmade shoes, and I don't think he would donate any money unless he thought it was well-spent.'

'I heard that he wants to see the site personally.'

Gloria had stayed silent too long, and now joined the conversation. 'Yes, it sounds like he intends to find time to pay us a visit. That's why we are trying to push progress with the first units, so that we have something to show him — perhaps enough for him to imagine what the whole site once looked like. Unfortunately, speed is never the friend of any archaeologist — you need to be patient and careful — but we are hoping to display some levels on at least one unit, so that we can explain and show him how it's done.'

Kim nodded. It wasn't a very high hill, but it was the highest spot in the area. She looked into the hazy distance, and tried to imagine what it had looked like when the whole area had been covered with trees and forests. Nowadays, farmland had taken over everywhere, and there were roads cutting determinedly into the landscape.

Uncle Jack had his hands crossed

behind his back. He said, 'Your chances of finding something worthwhile should be pretty good. This place was probably of special significance for the surrounding area for as long as humans have lived here. Superstitious priests probably held their ceremonies here. Saxons took over from the Romans and built here for a similar reason — it was a good strategic position.'

Alex asked Kim, 'Did you never go with your uncle when he was on his travels?'

She laughed softly. 'Not often. He usually went to outlandish places, and we had to go to school. There wasn't much for two young girls to do if we went along anyway, so after one or two trips we realized we were better off at home. He probably worried the whole time we were with him. Our schoolfriends envied us . . . But he never took us to hazardous places or anywhere he thought was dangerous. I remember a visit to Libya when it was still peaceful. We were out in the desert. It was quite special, and I loved it.'

Uncle Jack ran his hand through his grey hair. 'Yes, I remember it too. I can't remember how often I had to drag you inside to go to bed. You spent hours wrapped up in an old Bedouin blanket. How old were you?'

'I think I was about thirteen; Julie was eleven. I was fascinated by the desert, especially at night when the heavens were plastered with stars.'

Gloria joined in. 'I can't remember how often I was captivated by wherever we were. There was always a sense of adventure, the allure of the unknown, the attraction of somewhere that completely captured the imagination. I expect you felt the same, Alex, didn't you?'

'Yes, and I also understand why Kim found the desert so fascinating. There's never a day when the desert looks exactly as it did the day before, and the night sky is really something special. Absolute silence, or the merest sounds of the wind, are all you hear.' He exchanged a knowing look with Kim and smiled. Her spirits lifted.

Alex resumed: 'If you follow me, I'll take you across to the outer boundaries of our possible search area. We may not uncover all that's in between. It all depends on whether we discover something here. If we find enough to encourage us, we will extend the dig — until the money runs out.'

He led the way, and continued to give Kim an insight into the proposed happenings. He was an interesting guide, and didn't flower his speech with too many terms that she didn't understand. She guessed that it wasn't easy for him to come down to the level of a complete novice, but he managed it.

An hour later, they returned to the office. Both visitors refused the offer of coffee. Uncle Jack said, 'Thanks, my boy! It was an interesting insight. I'll look forward to hearing how you get on. I wish you luck!'

Alex nodded.

Kim added, 'Yes, thank you very much for taking time off to show us what's going on. I can understand much better now I've seen the actual site. It will help with my accounting.'

He gave her a smile. 'It was a pleasure. I'll be in touch with my first recorded list of supplies soon.'

Kim nodded, and as she viewed him, she was aware that her heartbeat increased noticeably. She felt confused by the unexpected reaction. She was almost glad to hear Gloria interrupt.

'I could have dealt with those lists for you, if someone had explained in advance what was wanted.'

Alex looked at Kim. 'Kim was especially employed to do it. I presume it was partly because she's a neutral person, and not directly associated with the actual excavation. I'm glad she's doing it. You and I have enough to do here onsite. We don't need the extra task of keeping detailed spending records: our time is better invested elsewhere.' He walked to the door and opened it. 'Have a safe journey. I'll see you soon, Kim. I hope to see you again before long too, Jack.'

'Any time, my boy. I'm usually buried in my papers, but I'm making good progress, and I'll always be glad to see you and chat about the dig, or about old times.'

Kim remembered to be polite and say, 'Thanks to you too, Gloria, of course.' Gloria nodded without replying.

They both agreed, as they made their way back to the car, that it had been an interesting visit and that Alex was a skilful guide.

6

Kim wasn't in the office when Alex came to leave the recorder. When Derek gave it to her and said Alex had come and gone, she felt a twinge of disappointment. She told herself not to be so silly.

Derek added, 'The visit from David Holland looks like it's on the books. Old Booth is already getting in a right dither about it.'

Kim laughed. 'Is he? Why? It's not his excavation site.'

Picking up one of the biscuits she had on a plate on her desk, he bit off a corner and sat down. 'I think he's trying to organize things so that he gets Holland here first to impress him, before he has to take him to the actual site later. Perhaps he's anxious to nail him for another donation.'

'He'll only put him off if he does.

How does he intend to get him here?'

'Apparently, by inviting him to lunch with some of the other university bigwigs.'

'I shouldn't think that David Holland wastes time on social lunches in his working time, but on the other hand . . . perhaps he likes being fawned on.'

Derek shrugged, and the second biscuit disappeared. 'I don't think he'll pull it off either, but I've given up battling with him. Why should I bother? When I get things right, it only adds more leaves to his laurel wreath, and he doesn't even notice.'

'Well, be careful! If he notices you're not smoothing his path, he might start shoving boulders in your way to block your own career.'

Derek got up. 'I realize that, love. I've already applied for a job at an American university. If I get it, I'll be beyond his reach. I'd like a change of scenery and a change of colleagues. You are one of the few normal human beings I talk to in this place. They're all either buried in their work, or busy planning how to get rid of someone else who's standing in their way on the ladder to success.'

She laughed. 'You know best. Good luck, if that's what you really want. If I was a permanent fixture, I'd be sorry to see you go, but I won't be here either in a couple of months' time. Until then, my lips are sealed.' As a last thought, Kim swivelled in her chair and added, 'If you hear of anyone who's looking for a secretary to do general office work, let me know, will you?'

'Will do!'

'Have you anything for me to do now?'

'I've got some boring lists and stuff for the history department to knock into shape.'

'Bring them over. It'll give me something to do this afternoon.'

'You are too good to be true! I will, with pleasure.'

Kim watched him leave with another biscuit in his hand, and felt sorry that his boss didn't appreciate his hard-working assistant. The fact that Derek was thinking of leaving the country made it even more depressing.

Two days later, Alan Booth himself came fussing around. 'Have you heard that David Holland is due? If he arrives on this side of the building, fetch me immediately!'

She nodded. 'I will. I didn't know he was coming today. Has he given you a definite time of arrival?'

Looking flustered, and wiping his brow with a capacious white handkerchief, he was clearly harassed. 'No. He's attending some company meeting nearby, and couldn't say what time he'd be here. He hoped it'd be between one and two o'clock. He refused my suggestion of lunch with some of the department heads, and said he'd have a cup of coffee with the team after he'd seen the site. I warned Alex's assistant to prepare sandwiches or titbits with the coffee. I hope she has enough sense not to offer him sandwiches the size of doorsteps.'

'I'm sure that Ms Thurston knows exactly what's appropriate. She seems to be a very efficient and capable assistant.'

'And she has an excellent degree! I wish Holland had time for a quick talk first, but it doesn't look like it.'

'Well, I expect he's very busy.'

'Yes, that's true. Don't forget to warn me if he happens to come in through this entrance! The minute he arrives!'

'Yes, of course, Mr Booth.' She was glad when he left. She understood why Derek was looking for another post. Mr Booth was puffed up with his own importance and had lost sight of reality.

She went on with her work, and looked up in surprise when, a short time later, the door burst open. A tall hefty man with a crewcut and shifty eyes checked the room before stepping to the side to make way for his boss. Kim recognized David Holland from the picture Linda had shown her. She got up.

He looked at ease and interested. His glance took in the surroundings, and he advanced with an outstretched hand. 'Good morning! I'm David Holland. I think I'm expected?'

'Yes, good morning Mr Holland! Mr Booth is expecting you. He wasn't sure which entrance you'd use. This is a side entrance, but I'll tell him you're here.' She indicated a nearby chair.

He smiled and shook his head. 'Blame my security people. They always keep me away from main entrances for safety reasons.' While Kim punched Mr Booth's extension number into the telephone, David asked, 'What do you do? Something to do with this dig?'

She told Mr Booth that Mr Holland had arrived, and then answered the question. 'I'm responsible for the bookkeeping side of the project, and if I have any more spare time, I do other work for the department.' Kim decided he must be an unusual man to ask who she was and what she did. She was a mere minion. Perhaps that was a reason he was so successful — he showed interest in everybody and everything.

He was an attractive man, and his smile didn't lessen his appeal. 'Really? Then I'm glad we came to your office. Have you any balance sheets I can look at while we're waiting?'

Kim hurried to hand him the latest one from a folder on the corner of her desk. He perused it without comment. She had the feeling he was so used to reading figures that he judged the situation at a glance. He handed it back.

'That looks okay to me. I'm glad someone is keeping an eye on things. Expenses can run out of control if no one checks now and then.'

She came to Alex's defence. 'I think Mr Harrison is used to controlling excavation expenses. This is not the first sponsored dig he's handled. I think my work is just relieving him of the bothersome bookkeeping he used to have to do. And, naturally, it provides you with immediate information about how your money is being spent.'

Shrewdly, he asked, 'And where do your wages come from?'

'A university sponsorship on a short-term basis. The university was anxious to be sure you'd have no regrets in donating your money, so they badgered other people to pay my wages!' She smiled at him.

'And what's your name?' His eyes twinkled.

'Kim, Kim Goddard.'

At that moment Mr Booth rushed in and took over. He welcomed their visitor with a prepared speech and offered him refreshments in his study. David waved the suggestion aside.

'I've had lunch at the company. I'd like to go straight to the excavation. I've a business dinner in London this evening, so I can't stay more than an hour or two before my helicopter picks me up. Is there a suitable landing place nearby?'

Mr Booth hurried to reply. 'There are fields all round the site. I'm sure you could use one of those.'

David nodded. 'Shall we leave? I think the site isn't far from here, is it?'

'No. It's about fifteen minutes away.'

'Let's go, then.' He turned to Kim. 'Why don't you join us? You're part of it too.'

Mr Booth looked irritated. She hurried to say, 'I've already been there.'

He brushed her dissent aside. 'Seeing it a second time won't harm you. It'd be nice to have someone else with me who also knows nothing about archaeology! Someone I can hold a normal conversation with.'

Kim could tell that he was a very rich, powerful, outspoken and honest man. Somehow, his complete honesty made him almost likeable. It was a feeling she had about Alex Harrison, too. Most likely David knew how to manipulate people, and didn't suffer fools gladly — Alex didn't, either. David Holland's approach had made him what he was — a commanding, influential individual.

Mr Booth gave up resisting as David Holland ushered her towards the door. She grabbed her linen jacket, and a pair of flat shoes that she kept in the bottom drawer of her desk, and went with him.

He gestured Mr Booth to the accompanying car. 'You can travel with my security people. Kim comes with me.'

There was no point in protesting. He already had his hand in the small of her back and was directing her to the back seat of his limousine. Kim tried to get into it as elegantly as was possible while wearing a buckskin skirt that skimmed her knees and a loose cream blouse. He grinned as he noticed. 'You have good legs; don't worry about putting them on show.'

He circled the vehicle and got in beside her. Kim remarked, 'I didn't expect to go anywhere this morning. The site director will definitely tell me my clothing is impractical.'

He shrugged. 'You came from your office at my invitation. You don't need to look like a hobo to tour an archaeological site, do you?'

Kim wondered if talking in platitudes was his method of flirting with any woman who crossed his path. She pushed her hair out of her face. 'A skirt is, without a doubt, impractical for visiting an archaeological site. Trousers are much better suited for such things.'

He leaned back and his arm slid across the back of the seat. Kim met the eyes of the chauffeur in the rear mirror. Was he used to his boss chatting up women in the back of the car? She felt uneasy with the thought. She slid further away from him, towards the window.

'Tell me about yourself.'

'Me? There's nothing much to tell. I'm sure you'd be bored.'

'I don't believe that. Everyone is special in some way. I gather your present job is temporary? It's just as well, believe me! From what I saw of Mr Booth, you'll wither and perish if you stay there too long. That place has nothing to do with real life.'

Kim found him disturbing because he was who he was; but he was also interesting and she liked the honesty in his eyes. She knew she was free to say what she liked. She'd never meet him again. 'Perhaps, but it does have a purpose. Without idealistic academics, the world would be very pragmatic and dull. Academics seem to live in a world of their own, but they do change things. I'm sure that most of them are not as dull and dry as you think.' She was thinking about Alex as she spoke. 'They want the same things from life as everyone else.

His eyes twinkled. 'And what would that be?'

'Happiness, satisfaction, security, a loving family background. The things money or bags of knowledge can't buy.'

'Are you referring to me? Do you think I don't want that?'

She met his glance. 'I don't know you, so I can't answer that. I've only read articles that suggest that making money is the most important thing in your life.'

He threw back his head and laughed. He was more serious, though his eyes twinkled, when he commented, 'They could be completely wrong, and I might want exactly the same things as you said.'

'I have no idea, but life is probably more complicated for prominent people. I imagine they can never be sure if people like them for themselves, or because they're rich and famous. People like you are automatically damned to live in a semi-artificial world. It must be hard to hold on to reality, and keep your feet on the ground.'

He was silent for a moment. 'You are an unusual woman, and you are spot on there. Now, tell me about yourself.'

Kim did. She told him about Uncle Jack and why she and Julie had grown up with him. She told him that her sister had a brain like a computer and was at university at present. She told him she'd like to do something special with her life one day, but hadn't decided what yet. She told him about the village and some of the people she knew there.

'So, your uncle is a geologist? That's not a run-of-the-mill profession these days. He took care of you and your sister when your parents died? That was very praiseworthy.'

'Yes, it was, because he was a bachelor and never married. We love him to bits, even though he's a bit of a scatterbrain.'

He chuckled. 'It sounds like you've already found some of the important things in life.'

'Yes, I think that's true. I'm happy with my life, my uncle, Linda — our former housekeeper — and my sister. They're people I can depend on and who care about me. I'm contented, even though a full-time steady job and more spare cash would be nice . . . but they're not essential for happiness.' They were nearing the excavation site.

'And what about a boyfriend, marriage, a family of your own?'

'I hope I'll meet the right person one day, but that's in the lap of the gods.'

He studied her face for a moment. 'I hope you find him.'

The car came to a stop and he hurried around to open the door and handed her out. Kim slid across the seat. She changed her shoes quickly, stuffed her heels into her bag, and then followed David. Alex came towards them with Gloria at his side. When he viewed them, his expression showed his surprise. It was immediately followed by another look, bordering on disapproval. Perhaps something had gone wrong on the site this morning, and David Holland's visit was getting in the way of progress. She looked away briefly, and didn't notice that Alex's expression was fixed on her and not on David Holland. Gloria's immediate gushing smile made up for Alex's hesitation until he remembered his manners and stuck out his hand.

'Good morning, Mr Holland. Welcome to the site. We haven't a great deal to show at present, but I hope you can get an idea of what we're excavating and how.' He gave Kim a stiff nod, but no word of greeting, as they were about to set off.

Mr Booth manoeuvred her aside and Kim presumed she could now fade into the background. She wondered how she could get back to the office.

Alex said. 'Follow me, everyone!'

David turned and beckoned to Kim. She coloured and made haste to join him. She felt embarrassed, but was hardly in a position to refuse. When Alex noticed, his expression stiffened again, but he turned away and carried on.

He showed David the recent units and explained where future sections were planned. Kim listened. David asked questions now and then. Alex told him much the same things that Kim had heard before, but added a bit more about the period when the

Romans had probably used the hill. People with their equipment of trowels and brushes were busy uncovering more of the units she'd seen previously. They were much deeper and there was something that looked like part of a wall. David was very interested and absorbed.

An hour later, they returned to the site office. Gloria, or someone else, had prepared small triangular sand-wiches and small vol-au-vents filled with chicken and shrimp. Coffee was also ready and waiting. Not knowing whether she was invited or not, Kim trailed along behind David and moved to the side once they were in the office.

The small room was full, and eventually she helped herself to a cup of coffee. David was talking to Alex. Alex's eyes met hers across the crowd. They looked stormy. David noticed the exchange, wondered what it was about, and was amused by his suppositions. He was good at reading hidden situations. Kim hoped the visit wasn't a flop.

Some minutes later, they shook hands and David moved towards the door. Everyone started to follow him like lemmings. Outside, people took leave of him, and he looked around and saw Kim. She was near the doorway and he came across.

'Bye Kim! I hope we meet again. Thanks for your philosophical views on life. I'll bear them in mind.'

She managed a smile. He was an unusual man. She was surprised he hadn't forgotten her already. She didn't think they'd meet again. Mr Booth would make sure she wasn't around if he ever came again. She liked him and wondered if he had any real friends. She felt sorry for him. Money wasn't always the answer.

'Don't pay any attention to me, I chatter too much. Good luck, and it was nice to meet you!'

He nodded. 'My car will take you back to your office. I don't need it any more today once I reach my helicopter. Wait here! I'll send it back for you.'

There was no point in arguing. She nodded. He turned away and strode determinedly to the waiting car. Everyone stood around watching until it left the site. They began to disperse again. Kim could tell Alex hadn't approved of her coming with David, but she had no intention of explaining why she was here. He wasn't her custodian. She leaned against the metal office wall to change her shoes. Her flat shoes were muddy now, but there was no way she could clean them apart from rubbing them briefly on some nearby grass. She held them in her hand and waited.

Gloria passed, and her glance slid down until she was viewing Kim's skirt. 'Rather unsuitable, isn't it? Or were you just hoping to attract our millionaire?'

Kim coloured. Alex was just a few steps behind her and must have heard her. He measured her up with another appraising look. Someone from the site caught up with them and grabbed his attention. Alex went off with the man in the direction they'd just come from without a farewell.

Kim wondered why she cared about what they thought of her, but she did. Gloria would probably fill his ears with nonsense: tell him that she had her eye on David Holland's money. She hated the idea that he'd get the wrong impression and think badly of her, but she couldn't do anything about it. She stared into empty air and then threw back her shoulders. She was glad when David's limousine returned.

She had the company of Mr Booth on the way back, but as he never made much effort to hold a normal conversation with her, she had plenty of time to look out at the passing scenery and remind herself that she would at least be able to impress Julie when she told her she'd actually met David Holland.

★   ★   ★

The following weekend, Alex called at the cottage. It was a wonder that Uncle Jack heard the doorbell, but he was on his way to the kitchen at that moment for something to eat. When he opened the door, he was genuinely pleased to see the visitor, and gestured him inside.

'Alex! What's brought you here?'

'I was just passing, and thought I'd drop in and ask how your report is getting on.'

Uncle Jack nodded. 'Fine, fine! I'm already on my last conclusions. Come in! What about you? How's the dig going?'

Alex looked around. 'Not too bad; we've found bits of pottery, but nothing sensational so far. Still, even shards like that give us hope that we'll find more interesting stuff if we carry on.'

'Would you like a coffee? Kim left me a vacuum flask filled up to the brim. I only need to get you a cup or a mug.'

He looked round gingerly. 'Kim isn't in?'

'No, she's gone out with Nigel. I

think she mentioned some event where they intend to roll cheeses down a hillside or some other silly nonsense.'

'Nigel? Is he someone special?'

Leading the way into the living room, Uncle Jack uttered, 'Not as far as I know, but I don't pry into the girls' lives. Nigel comes from the village. His father is vicar of the next parish. His dad and I belong to the chess club. Nigel is okay, although I think he's not right for Kim.' He went to the sideboard and a group of decanters and glasses. 'Let's have a proper drink and then you can tell me the latest. Whiskey or grappa?'

'I shouldn't, I'm driving; but a small grappa will be okay.'

Uncle Jack busied himself with their drinks. Alex studied the pictures on the mantelpiece, and his glance lingered on one of the two sisters, arms entwined and laughing.

7

Julie shrieked. 'Really? You've got an invitation to David Holland's party and you can take someone with you?'

'Yep! I was flabbergasted when it arrived. I even thought about turning it down — I haven't spent more than two hours with the man, and yet he's still invited me to a garden party at his country home. Uncle Jack isn't interested, and Linda said she'd only come if she could sit down all day. I know how much you'd enjoy it, so I phoned and asked if I could bring my sister. The toffee-nosed secretary said I could bring anyone I liked. I knew you'd jump at the chance. From what I gather, it's a very informal party. Lots of business acquaintances sprinkled with some people he knows more personally.'

'And party dresses?'

'Well, I didn't ask, but as it takes place late afternoon, I think a dress would be suitable, don't you? I have no idea what's expected. There was no mention of preferred dress on the invitation, so it can't be very formal.'

'Oh, goodie! I bought a brilliant dress last week, in the end of season sales. I thought it would be super for the end-of-term ball when I saw it on the rack, but it's perfect for a posh afternoon party too. It's sea-green. The material floats around me as I move.'

Kim laughed. 'It sounds like a humdinger, and just right for your colouring. You'll look like a sea-nymph, I expect.'

'What will you wear?' Julie was silent for a moment. 'You can borrow it if you like, it'd look good on you too. I'll find something else. You're the one he invited, not me.'

'I thought I'd wear that bronze sheath dress, the one I wore at Stella's wedding.'

'Oh, yes! It looks great on you, and

suits you down to a T; but you should use more make-up.'

'Uh-uh! You know that's not my thing. Some foundation, a little more eyeshadow and a suitable lipstick will be enough. I'll never feel happier with more than that.'

'You have to make the best of what you have. When is it exactly? I'm going to mark the day on my calendar with a big red circle.

'It's next Friday at his home. Can you make it? We can have the Jeep and drive there; I've already cleared that with Uncle Jack. I've found out where it is and how to get there. It will take roughly an hour from here.'

Kim could hear Julie clapping her hands. 'Of course I can! I'd even abandon lectures to do so, but that won't be necessary. I've an early lecture on Friday morning, so I can be home before lunch. It's so exciting! Fancy me meeting David Holland! He's good-looking and rich, and just up my street!'

Thinking about all the tittle-tattle in the newspapers and magazines, Kim didn't want to dampen her sister's fun, but she hoped Julie understood that David Holland could eat her for breakfast and spit out her bones without a qualm. The papers painted him as a known womaniser. An easily-impressionable young student in her second year at university would present him with no problem if he zoomed in on her. On the other hand, there would undoubtedly be lots of other beautiful women there and, as pretty as Julie was, she probably couldn't compete with the kind of sophisticated ladies David knew and favoured.

'Julie! He's a flirt and a lady-killer! He is not anything like the kind of man you've met until now. It would be silly of you to think you can handle him — you can't. I saw enough of him to know he's the type of man who expects sex without any strings attached. Check the Internet for the horde of women he's been involved with! Undoubtedly a lot of them also thought that he liked them for who they were.'

'Kim, I'm not stupid: I realize that! He won't give either of us a second glance because we're not in his league, but it is exciting to be invited to one of his parties, isn't it? How did you manage to merit an invite?'

'I'm not sure. I only spent about fifteen minutes alone with him in his car on the way to the dig. I must admit, once I'd conquered my initial nervousness, I quite enjoyed talking to him. He was very honest. Perhaps he doesn't get the chance to talk to many ordinary people any more, and that's why he remembered my name when he listed names for the invitations.'

'Did he flirt with you?'

'No! At first I thought he might try, but we had quite a normal chat. Perhaps all the negative reports in the newspapers about him are exaggerated. I haven't made up my mind yet. He does have an aura of authority and control about him, but that isn't surprising when you realize what he's achieved and what he stands for.'

'He's had a head-start in life, though, hasn't he? His father has a title, he went to all the right schools and universities, and he had a financial springboard. Nevertheless, it'll be great if I just got to shake his hand. It'd be a feather in my cap, and something I can impress my fellow students with!'

Kim laughed softly and felt calmer. Julie realized she wasn't going to be Cinderella meeting Prince Charming. It meant they could enjoy finding out how the other half lived for a couple of hours.

The following Friday, Uncle Jack viewed them, his glasses resting on his forehead. 'I must say, you both look very beautiful. Enjoy yourselves — and drive carefully, Kim!'

'I will. I expect we'll be back early enough to share supper. If not, there's some cold chicken in the fridge, and you can either microwave some chips or heat up the mash that's left over from yesterday.'

'Don't worry about me, I won't starve. Enjoy yourselves.'

Julie skipped towards the door and her dress floated and drifted along with her. It suited her blonde hair and turquoise-blue eyes to perfection. Watching her, Kim thought she had never seen her look prettier. She was pleased with her own appearance too. The bronze dress emphasized her colouring. The simple style skimmed her figure and fitted beautifully. When she'd bought it for a friend's wedding, she'd immediately loved the style. It was timeless in its lines and colour, and that made it one of her favourite things.

There were security people confirming people's invites when they pulled up in front of some large wrought-iron gates. They were checked and waved through. The gravelled driveway, up to the facade of an impressive, elegant Georgian mansion house, was bordered with ancient trees. Cars were parked in a field on the side.

Their Jeep stood out among the rows of classy, sleek limousines and convertibles. Julie looked at her sister as they got out. Her eyes twinkled and the corners of her mouth were turned up. 'Well, we certainly won't have any trouble finding it later on, will we? It's the oldest, oddest, and shoddiest vehicle of the whole lot.'

Kim joined in with her laughter and they linked arms.

They followed a loose straggle of other people who were climbing the steps of an impressive portico. A stiff butler stood just inside the open door. Checking people's invitations as they arrived, he crossed the names off his list one by one. Now and then he knew the people, and nodded or said something briefly before they moved on. When it was their turn, he viewed them with fleeting interest and indicated towards an open door straight ahead of them. 'Mr Holland is in the sitting room, the conservatory, or perhaps in the garden.

Carry on and help yourself to refreshments.'

They did as they were told. They glanced at each other and were silently impressed by the beautiful proportions of the large entrance hall. A grand staircase faced them; its sides bordered with intricate black wrought-iron work. A flight of wide marble steps rose to a mid-level landing, parted to the left and the right, and then continued upwards to the next floor. The elegance of the Georgian period was evident in the whole appearance of the place — the elaborate plasterwork, the long eight-paned windows, and the niches around the hallway housing classical statues. Their high heels echoed on the black-and-white marble floor, and they paused to look around.

Julie said, 'What a beautiful room!'

Kim jumped when she heard David Holland's voice right behind her. She didn't see where he came from. His words floated over her shoulder. 'Yes, it is, isn't it? Hello, Kim!' He turned to

Julie and gave her a smile. 'Who is this?'

'Hello, David. Thank you for the invitation. This is my sister, Julie.'

He nodded, and his firm mouth curled on the edge of a smile. He gestured around the hallway. 'The only thing that's not perfect in this house is how much it costs to keep it in a good condition!'

Julie retorted, 'You shouldn't think about the drawbacks. It is such a beautiful place, just be glad that you own it.'

He looked surprised, but after regarding her for a second, he said, 'Yes, you're right. You are like your sister and her attitude to life and possessions, aren't you? The two of us had a bit of a chat in the car the other day. It was stimulating.'

Julie looked up and there was a moment of silence as their eyes met. 'Yes, I know. She told me.'

'And what do you do?'

Julie was confident enough to not feel overwhelmed by his presence. 'I'm at university. My main subjects are mathematics and computer sciences, but I'm doing a couple of other subjects too. Otherwise I'd get bored.'

'Mathematics is not everyone's cup of tea.'

'No, but I love it. At school I usually grasped things very fast, and I think I understood things better than my teachers most of the time.'

His brows lifted and he laughed softly. 'Really? Then you certainly are unusual.' He turned to Kim. 'If you go straight ahead, you'll find something to drink and some nibbles. I've got to circulate among the other guests but I hope we'll meet again later on. I'm really glad you could make it, and that you've brought such a charming companion.' He left them and walked towards someone who had just passed the butler's check-in.

Kim and Julie walked into the sitting room where various tempting food was arranged on large silver trays and positioned throughout the room on side-tables. Several servants were circling the room with trays of drinks. Julie loaded a plate, and took a serviette.

'Come on! We won't get anything as good as this for a while again. This looks like caviar. I've never had any before, have you?' She took a bite. 'Not bad! Oh look, smoked salmon. I really love that, and I buy it when my monthly allowance arrives, but I can't afford it as often as I'd like.'

Kim smiled softly. 'I should hope not. You're a student. If you could afford smoked salmon regularly, it would mean your allowance was too generous. Remember, we don't get it at home often, either! That's what makes it special. If you had it every day, then it wouldn't be.'

Julie took a glass of champagne from one of the passing servants. 'Help yourself, Kim. It's bound to be real champagne, not the sparkling wine we're used to.' She lifted her glass towards her sister. 'This is the life!'

The serving woman grinned and said

softly, 'Yes, it is the real stuff, and you can have as much as you like.'

Kim helped herself to a glass. 'Don't encourage her, please, or I'll have to carry her home! I can afford one glass, but no more. I'm driving.'

They didn't know anyone else, so they wandered side by side, admired the house and drifted through a long orangery out into the garden. Decorated tables and chairs were dotted here and there on the lawns and near the flowerbeds. In the distance there was a slate-coloured river, and beyond that rolling farmland. From where they stood, the animals grazing in the fields looked like toy miniatures.

'Gosh! Do you think it all belongs to David Holland?'

Kim nodded. 'I expect so. He has to invest his money somewhere, and buying up the surrounding countryside is also a great method of ensuring his privacy, isn't it? In a way, it's sad that he has to cut himself off from everyday life.'

Julie looked around. 'I've never

thought about it, but I suppose prominent people do live in a kind of golden cage, don't they? On the other hand, you have to take the good with the bad. You can't have it both ways.' She put her glass down on a nearby sill. 'I need to find the Ladies. Coming?'

'No, I'm fine. If you stopped guzzling champagne, you wouldn't need to go so often. Ask one of the serving people where the cloakroom is. I'll wait for you here.'

Kim stood at the top of the steps leading down from the terrace to the garden below. The afternoon sunlight struck the paved stonework and splashed the walls with flashes of illumination here and there. With a long-stemmed crystal glass in her hand, she watched as some of the people wandering between well-ordered flowerbeds and strategically-placed greenery and trees. Her contemplation was disturbed when David Holland touched her arm.

'There you are! I've been trying to

find you! I just met your sister again, and I asked her if she'd like to see the rest of the house. She said she'd love to, but also that she'd promised to come back to you on the terrace. I left her looking for the cloakroom, and came to tell you she'll be back later.' He gave her a disarming smile. 'You're welcome to join us if you like.'

There was something in his expression that told her he hoped to be alone with Julie. Unintentionally, her sister had worked her magic on him. Nervousness ruffled through Kim. She was his guest, but her protective instincts were stronger.

'I expect your attention flatters her, and she's impressed by your authority and possessions. She's sometimes easily carried away, and is too enthusiastic. I love my sister, David, and I think she's too young to grasp the consequences if you wrap her round your little finger. I hope that you realize that she's very impressionable.' She added quickly, 'And please don't think I'm saying that because I'm green-eyed, or anything like that. I'm just wary of anything or anyone that could hurt her.'

He looked taken aback for a moment, but then he laughed out so loud, so heartily that people standing nearby turned to watch them. He tucked his hand under her elbow and guided her away from the throng to a spot further along the terrace where it was a lot quieter. 'Kim, I have no treacherous or wicked intentions. I admit that I find your sister refreshingly direct, and she's exceptionally beautiful. I can also tell that she's bursting with energy and is full of passion and determination. She is also completely unaware of how beautiful she is. Of course, I'm attracted to her — but today my intentions are perfectly honourable, I promise! You shouldn't believe all the rubbish you read in the newspapers about me. Three-quarters of the stuff is made up.'

Feeling uncomfortable with the situation, Kim managed a few other remarks. 'And the other quarter? She's the only family I have, apart from Uncle Jack, and I'd hate to see her unhappy. She's a brilliant mathematician, and people forecast a dazzling future for her. She is also a generous, fun-loving person. Sometimes I worry because she runs head-first into whatever appeals to her.'

He nodded and they were silent for a moment. 'You are both unusual women, and just because you are a year or two older doesn't mean you are responsible for your sister. I don't know her properly, but I think she knows what she's doing, and is quite capable of making sensible decisions. I think you underestimate her ability to recognize danger.'

She took a deep breath and nodded. 'You're right!'

He leaned forward and kissed her on her cheek. 'I promise that I do not intend to drag her into my den and show her my etchings! I'll bring her back safe and sound. Or will you change your mind and come with us after all?'

'No, go ahead. I know I'm being silly. I just wanted you to know how I felt. I'm perfectly fine here. It's such a lovely view, and the weather is perfect too. Julie is much more interested in historical places than I am. I'll wander around and meet her here later.'

'Right!' He turned to leave, and while doing so he noticed other people coming up the steps from the garden.

Kim reasoned they had probably seen her with David as they approached. Alex looked disgruntled. Gloria looked happier, and had her arm tucked into his.

David lifted his hand. 'Hi, Alex! And Gloria . . . that was the name, wasn't it? Glad you came. I have to disappear for a while, but in the meantime perhaps you can keep Kim company?' He hurried off, leaving Kim to see that Alex wasn't happy with the idea. Gloria was stuck to his side like chewing gum to a shoe sole. She longed to move away, but she remained static and tongue-tied. She hoped her expression didn't show her nervousness.

Even though something had clearly displeased him, Alex managed to sound quite composed. 'It's nice to see you here too.'

She met his glance and lost herself in the blue of his eyes. 'I was surprised to get an invitation, but it looks like David Holland is more magnanimous than the press make him out to be.'

Gloria tugged at his arm. 'Why don't we join the others?' She looked very smart, in a tight-fitting pink linen costume that suited her. Blondes always looked good in pink, and Gloria had good dress sense and knew exactly what to wear to her advantage.

Kim told herself to stop looking for something to criticise. What did it matter if Gloria was with Alex? It was nothing to do with her.

But she had to admit that she was finding it impossible to ignore the attraction whenever she met Alex. She'd have to pull herself together and pay less heed to him and what he was doing. The wind had ruffled his hair. He was wearing a classic dark blue suit with a white shirt and a faintly-patterned grey-and-blue tie. She had never seen him in conventional clothes before. They merely increased his attractiveness to her.

She said, 'Go ahead! I've promised to wait for David and my sister. He's showing her round the house.'

Alex looked disinterested. 'Right! If you're okay on your own . . . ' His voice was brusque and final. 'Let's join the others and get ourselves something to eat.' In Kim's direction, he added, 'Enjoy yourself!'

Before she could reply, he'd turned abruptly and walked towards the open French windows. Gloria looked rather surprised, but gave Kim a weak smile and hurried after him.

Kim felt glum. Alex wasn't obliged to chat with her, but clearly he couldn't wait to get away. She thought they were at least friends — especially since he'd called at the cottage a couple of times. Perhaps he was a snob after all, and didn't think David should have singled her out and included her in such an illustrious gathering. She gripped her glass tightly and shrugged. What did it matter what he thought, or what he said? When all was said and done, they were merely passing acquaintances.

8

She adjusted her shoulder bag, went down the steps, and skirted the edge of the garden. She heard wild pigeons cooing in the nearby wood, and there was the smell of sunned grasses in the air. Looking back at the facade of the house, she admired the simplicity of its beautiful lines. There was a wood straggling alongside the tidy lawns and flowerbeds. The thicket of thickly clustered pines was dark and impenetrable. A glance within told her anyone would need an axe to hack through all the low bushes and dead stuff to get to its centre.

She tried to ignore her thoughts about Alex and Gloria, but it wasn't easy. Her interest in Alex couldn't be easily forgotten. There was something about the man that stirred her awareness a great deal more than she wanted it to. Every time she saw him, something flickered within her. It was obvious that he wasn't interested in her. Were her feelings for him a kind of hero-worship? Up till now, she'd been free of emotional involvement, so she didn't want to spend her time thinking about him . . . but she couldn't stop doing so. There was no reason they'd ever meet again when her contract ended. She straightened her shoulders and admitted that she liked Alex, but didn't love him.

The sun was high, and a little breeze swept through the garden as she wandered. She concentrated on studying the purple shadows in the folds and hollows of the fields far away. Some people she passed nodded to her politely, but Kim was glad she was alone with the silence. It gave her time to adjust, to admit that he didn't belong to her world — and never would.

She concentrated on the garden party. Perhaps such functions were enjoyable if you were with people you knew. As far as she was concerned, there'd been nothing she wanted to remember about this afternoon.

She circled the area of the garden nearest to the house, and then sat on the parapet waiting for Julie. Through the open French window, she saw Alex and Gloria among a group of other people from the excavation. She could have joined them if she'd wanted to, but she didn't. Derek spotted her and came outside.

'Hi there! Come and join us!'

She shook her head. 'Hi! No, thanks — I'm waiting for my sister.'

He looked around. 'Quiet an exclusive do, isn't it? I'm surprised Holland bothered to invite us.'

She laughed softly. 'Well, that's definitely true as far as I'm concerned. I'm only a humble office worker. At least all the rest of you are academics with degrees. Who did you bring?'

He looked at her speculatively and remarked, 'A degree doesn't make you a better person; but, in contrast, nice people stay nice and are interesting characters. I brought Holly, the girl in the yellow dress. She's my girlfriend.' He looked along the terrace. 'Hey, here comes Holland. Is that your sister by his side? You mentioned you were bringing her.'

'Yes, that's Julie.'

'Wow! She's a sight for sore eyes, isn't she? And you said she has a brilliant brain too?'

'Yes, so I'm told. For maths and computers and suchlike! She's still at university, with at least another year to go.'

David brought Julie back to her sister's side. He nodded to Derek. 'You're someone else involved in this dig, aren't you?'

'In a loose sense. I'm like Kim. Working in the background and doing other things at the same time.'

Julie's eyes sparkled. 'The house is amazing, Kim. Full of beautiful furniture, and the bathrooms are absolutely fabulous.' David eyed her indulgently.

Kim nodded. 'If the inside is as lovely as the outside, I can imagine what it's like.'

David asked, 'I hope you've all had something to eat and drink?'

'Of course!'

'Good! Well, I must wander around and talk to some other guests. Enjoy the rest of the afternoon, and I hope to see you all again.'

Was it Kim's imagination, or did she notice fleeting disappointment on Julie's face? She understood why. Julie was probably overawed, but he wasn't the right kind of man for her. He was at least ten years older, and sophisticated and refined. Julie was still finding her feet in the adult world. She noticed Derek's girlfriend was looking wistfully in their direction, so she reminded him and he left them, saying, 'If you won't join us, I'll see you Monday, Kim! Bye, Julie!'

'Yes, till Monday!'

Julie watched him return to the

others. 'Are all those on this archaeo-logical dig? Why didn't you join them? I recognize that archaeologist you men-tioned. He's better-looking than in the picture we saw.'

'I didn't particularly want to join them. Derek just came over. He and I get on quite well.'

'And Mr Archaeology?'

'I don't think he likes me much, and I'm beginning to think I should reciprocate the feeling and ignore him.'

Julie shrugged. 'Let's go and look for another glass of bubbly, then!'

Kim laughed and tucked her arm through her sister's. 'One more glass for you, an orange juice for me. Tell me about your guided tour. You were quite honoured. I don't think he's spent as much time with anyone else since we arrived.' Kim deliberately avoided look-ing in the direction of the other dig workers when they moved, and she searched for one of the attendants circling the rooms with trays. 'What do you think of him?'

Julie sounded breathless. 'He's not at all like I expected him to be. Like you said, he seems to be very direct and honest. You can tell that he comes from a very cultivated background, but he's not stuck-up or snobbish. He's very attractive to look at, too, don't you agree?'

Kim nodded, but didn't comment. It was clear that David had made a strong impression on her sister. Generally, even when she'd just met someone, Julie found something to criticize. Kim thought it was because Julie believed it was important to have a boyfriend when you were a twenty-year-old student, but that it didn't mean you had to be in love with them. Kim had heard no criticism about David Holland, so her antennae sent her warning signals.

Julie gushed. 'He's very amusing and an interesting man. He's utterly charming! We didn't talk much about his work. Neither of us mentioned it. He told me about his family and how he'd grown up. He has two sisters. They're both older and married with children. His parents are nagging him to find someone to waltz down the aisle with, and then produce an heir to the family title.'

They found a tray loaded with drinks, and helped themselves to what they wanted. Kim said cautiously, 'He doesn't have a blameless reputation as far as women are concerned. He's a sophisticated man, and he's very rich. Women probably run after him all the time.'

Julie took a generous sip of her champagne. She tossed her blonde hair, and her expression grew fiercer. 'I don't believe all the nonsense that's written about him. Not now that I've talked to him.'

Kim changed the subject. 'Do you want to wander around the garden? You've already seen more of the house than most of the guests here today, and I don't mind if you do.'

Julie hugged her. 'This hasn't been

much fun for you, has it? Sorry, I've been selfish, and you haven't done anything except traipse around the greenery on your own. Let's go! I expect Uncle Jack is looking forward to hearing what it was like.'

'I didn't expect to be the belle of the ball. I don't mind being on my own. I'm fine. Linda wants to see you before you leave on Sunday morning.'

Julie finished her glass in one gulp. 'I intended to call around sometime tomorrow anyway. I'm quite ready to go if you are.'

Kim was glad. The sooner they left, the quicker she'd forget about Alex, and get things into perspective again. It wasn't just Julie who was letting her fancy run wild about a man. Gloria was clearly enamoured of Alex, and what was there to stop them pairing up? There was little doubt from the way he'd dodged Kim's company that he didn't intend to waste time on her. Ignoring him should be easy if she remembered that.

They found the Jeep easily. Most of the visitors' cars were still lined up. Kim had trouble getting out of the space because someone else had parked so haphazardly. Once they were bowling down the driveway, Julie looked back at the house. She said wistfully, 'It really is a gem of a place. Really lovely!'

'I gather that this is his home, and not the family seat — as the posh people say!'

Julie laughed. 'Dead right. His father's place is in Gloucester. Thanks for taking me along with you.'

Kim noted how much Julie had discovered in such a short time. She looked across briefly. 'You're welcome. I can't think of anyone I'd rather have with me, and David singled you out for special attention. I expect a lot of the women were jealous.'

'You should have come on the tour with us. I'm sure you would have enjoyed it. David told me he asked you to come.'

'Yes, he did, but I enjoyed the walk

just as much. I'm afraid that Uncle Jack won't be having anything half as high-class for his supper as what we've just seen back there.'

Julie quipped, 'I don't think he'd notice if we gave him a plate of stewed radishes. He doesn't seem to notice what he eats most of the time, does he?' She looked out of the passing scenery. 'I'll pop around to see Linda tomorrow morning, and I want to see Lucy before I go back. I haven't seen either of them for ages. I miss Linda's sensible comments.'

★　★　★

The next couple of weeks passed quietly. Kim didn't have to wonder how to deal with Alex when he turned up in her office. He was too busy on the site to waste time personally delivering his Dictaphone. When it was next full, he sent Gloria to deliver it one morning.

She looked around. 'So this is where you work?' She put the recorder down on the top of a filing cabinet. 'It's a lot quieter here than it is on site.'

'I expect it is.' Kim had no reason to be unfriendly. 'Would you like a cup of coffee?'

'No, thanks. I have to go into town. We need some bits and pieces fast. Alex asked me to drop that off on the way, and pick up a new one.'

Kim handed her the empty Dictaphone. She stuffed it into her bag. 'Someone mentioned this is only a temporary job for you. What will you do later on?'

'I don't know. I'm keeping my eyes open. Some kind of secretarial work.'

'Is your uncle still at home? Alex mentioned he'd visited him one Saturday morning recently.'

Kim was surprised. She knew nothing about Alex's visit. She tried not to sound taken aback. 'My uncle didn't mention that he'd called. Evidently I was out at the time.' She added, 'I finished typing my uncle's report one evening this week. He'll be off again in a month or two. He's been asked to do a study somewhere in Venezuela.'

Gloria nodded. 'He's a wanderer, isn't he? Alex and I are like that too.'

Curiosity got the better of her. 'Have you been on many digs together?'

'A couple. Alex is a very inspiring leader. He can motivate people to do their very best when they're on site with us. People who know nothing about it seem to think an archaeological dig is romantic. It isn't. It's back-breaking work, and you also have to be extremely careful. Every sweep of the brush, every scratch with the trowel, can reveal something. You can easily overlook something terribly important, or even damage something vital.'

'Have you found anything worthwhile yet?'

'Lots of pottery shards, and a couple of Saxon coins. We're not deep enough yet to expect much in the way of Roman finds. Alex is optimistic enough to expand the number of units, though. He's well-known for picking the right spots on a limited budget. I'm sure the best is yet to come.' She smiled.

'I hope so.'

'We all do.' Gloria brushed a nonexistent thread from her formal charcoal trousers. 'I'm so happy to be here, and part of Alex making his next great discoveries. Has David Holland been in touch?' Her expression was quite innocent. 'You seemed good friends the afternoon of the party. Even Alex noticed it.'

'No, I haven't heard from him, and I don't expect to. I send him regular updated reports of how the money is being spent to his office as he requested. I've never received any kind of acknowledgement. Most likely he's too busy to be bothered with such petty things, as long as we stick to the budget.'

Gloria nodded and looked at her watch. 'Yes, you're probably right. It is a new experience for Alex to be under constant financial control, but he's coping. Once he's put his mind to something, he makes it work, whatever it is. Well, I'll be off.'

'Bye! Thanks for the Dictaphone, and say hello to Alex from me.'

Gloria repositioned her bag and said, 'Will do! Bye!'

Kim thought she'd been almost friendly today. Perhaps she'd misjudged her.

The next time the recorder turned up, Alex brought it to the office himself, but she'd been out at the time. She just found a note saying that he'd taken the empty recorder that he'd found on the corner of the desk, and hoped it was okay. His message continued: *If it's not right, I'll send someone to exchange it for the right one. Let me know!*

It wasn't necessary. She entered all the details from the full one and cleared it again, leaving it lying where he'd found the other.

Sometimes she listened to him speaking the same text several times. She didn't know why she did so, but he had a pleasant voice, and somehow it made her feel good to hear him. She didn't crumple his note and throw it in the wastepaper basket, either. She smoothed it out and put it in the top drawer of her desk.

A week later, Derek suddenly burst into her office. 'They've made some really interesting discoveries at the site! They found some Saxon coins the other day — you already know about that, don't you?' She nodded. 'Well, when they went deeper, they found lots of shards of Roman tiles and the remains of a wall. Following along that, they think they've come to the bathhouse. They started some new units where Alex guessed the Commandant's House should be, and they've just reported that they found a hoard of coins. Probably buried by someone when there was growing insecurity and increasing danger in the region. Quite an interesting cache, apparently. They've also found some fragments of an inscription on a tablet near where they reckon the southeast gate was. That helps to establish where the other gates probably were, and will speed things up. The shortened form of the inscription is *Imperatori Caesari Divi Nervae Filio Nervae Traiano Augusto Germanico Dacico.*'

'And what does that mean?'

''For the Emperor Caesar Nerva Trajan Augustus, conqueror of Germany, conqueror of Dacia, son of the deified Nerva.' They are looking for the rest of the tablet, and perhaps others like it. It seems very likely that there was a tablet at each of the four gates. There are corners missing from this one, and they are still hoping to find them. It helps date when the fort was occupied — between A.D. 103 and 111.'

'Where was Dacia?'

'Romania.'

She nodded. She was delighted for Alex — and all the rest of the team, but especially for Alex.

Derek smiled. 'Mr Booth is preening like a cock in a farmyard, of course

— as if he'd found the stuff himself! He's busy trying to contact David Holland to tell him all about it. I think that Holland may make an effort to come and take another look, now they have some real finds to show him.'

'He'll be pleased to hear he hasn't contributed his money to a project with nothing to show for it in the end.'

'I bet he knew that Alex wouldn't touch a project with a bargepole unless he thought there was a good chance of success. Alex has a great reputation, and he's not interested in endangering that in any way.'

David did make a flying visit, and even called at her office to see her after he'd been to the site. She was genuinely pleased to see him. He must have a tight schedule every day, and an unplanned visit would mean a lot of switching and swapping.

'I wondered if I'd see you there, but Alex said he hadn't seen you for a couple of weeks. Don't you want to be in at the kill?'

She shook her head and smiled. 'You forget that I'm not important; I'm just an office minion. I'm pleased for them, of course, and I expect you are too?'

'Yes, good publicity! The finds are quite impressive. It's amazing the hoard of coins wasn't found by anyone, even if it was hidden in the wall. Whoever put it there was probably killed during an attack in this spot, or perhaps somewhere else.' He jingled his car keys, so Kim surmised he'd driven there himself. 'Alex has a theory that a lot of local residents may have DNA that would match that of those long-ago Romans. It would be interesting to find that out.'

Kim laughed softly. 'I wouldn't be surprised to find people would volunteer, but a lot would be very suspicious.'

He paused. 'You must take a look at the finds before they disappear to some museum.'

'It's not important for me to see them. Derek, Mr Booth's assistant, keeps me up to date. I'm just pleased for your sake and Alex's that it hasn't been in vain.'

'And they're far from finished yet. Who knows if they'll find lots of other artefacts? How's Julie?'

'She's fine.' Kim was a little surprised that he remembered her sister's name so easily.

'She's at the local university, isn't she?'

'Yes.'

He eyed her carefully. 'Would you object if I phoned her and asked her out for a meal? I know you're sceptical, and I understand why, but I have no intention of leading her astray. I enjoyed being with Julie that afternoon, and that doesn't happen to me very often anymore. My money and social standing blinds nearly all the women I ever meet to normal behaviour. I could tell Julie didn't give a scrap for all that hot air, and you don't care either. You only worry that she could get overwhelmed if I did set out to impress her, am I right?'

She nodded. 'I trust her judgement, but you must admit you come from a different world, and anyone would be impressed. You're also very strong-minded and determined, I don't know if that would be good for Julie.'

He nodded. 'I know what you mean. I'm afraid those characteristics have grown stronger through the years. When you run such a huge complex of businesses and other things like I do, you have to be stubborn and unbend-able sometimes. Being determined is not always a sign of a bad character.'

'No, I realize that, but on a personal level there has to be give and take. If one partner is too dominant, the other will be crushed in time.'

He nodded. 'Will you give me her telephone number?'

Kim met his glance. There was something pleading in his expression, and she liked him. She dithered for a moment, but then decided that if she refused him, she was taking control of Julie's life, and no one had the right to do that. Julie was already a lot more experienced in handling men than she was, and she had the feeling the attraction between the two was mutual. It was best to leave it in the lap of the gods.

She wrote Julie's number down on a scrap of paper and gave it to him. He looked pleased, like someone who'd succeeded in getting his favourite sweets at the tuck-shop. Perhaps he was more interested in Julie than she'd imagined.

He waved the paper. 'Thanks! I hope that she's free.'

'Don't you have to return to London?'

He grinned. 'That depends on whether Julie is free or not.' He glanced at his watch. 'You must go to the excavation site and see what they're doing. It is very, very interesting.'

'Perhaps!' Kim didn't think she'd go again unless she was invited. Alex seemed to want to ignore her as much as possible, and she didn't intend to go anywhere she wasn't wanted. 'If you see Julie, give her my love, and tell her to phone us. We haven't heard from her for days. Uncle Jack keeps asking after her.'

'Will do, if I see her.'

Kim had to resist the urge to phone her sister to find out if David had contacted her, and if they'd gone out together. She didn't, and reasoned that she had to stop behaving like a mother hen. Julie did phone, but she was out shopping at the time, and Uncle Jack merely reported that she said everything was fine — and she'd sounded quite chirpy.

9

A day or two later, Kim met Nigel in the village. He looked uncomfortable when she mentioned she hadn't heard from him for a while, and asked if anything was wrong.

He started to explain. 'I've been intending to phone you.' He moved from one foot to the other. 'But I felt awkward, and kept putting it off.'

Kim was puzzled. 'Why? We've known each other all our lives. There's no reason for you to feel uneasy about anything. What's wrong?'

He looked down at his shoes. 'Well, to put it bluntly, I met a girl at a social get-together in the parish hall. It was one of my father's dos, and I thought it would be the usual boring evening, but it wasn't. Ellie's aunt brought her along, and she wasn't exactly over the moon about being there either. We sort of drifted together and started talking . . . '

' . . . and you liked each other so much, you decided to meet again, and it's gone from there?' Kim smiled and touched his arm. 'It's fine, Nigel. You don't need to feel awkward at all! We were never girlfriend and boyfriend in that sort of way, were we? I'm really pleased you've met someone special. Ellie must be a very nice person.'

His face lightened. 'You don't mind?'

'No of course not. I'd like to meet her, and soon.'

'Whew! I was worried about telling you. I'm sure that you'll like Ellie. She's quiet and pretty, and I feel so right when we are together. We have a lot in common.'

Kim laughed softly. 'She sounds perfect for you. You are silly to think I'd object. I've always been grateful for our friendship, and I hope we'll stay friends, but I never thought of you in a romantic way — and you didn't think about me like that either. We were good substitutes, weren't we?'

He nodded. 'I suppose so.'

'Well, stop worrying, and be happy that you've found someone you really like at last.' She kissed his cheek. 'I have to go; I have to catch the post before today's final collection is due. Keep in touch; and next time you and Ellie are in the neighbourhood, call in and have a cup of tea!'

Nigel looked a lot happier. 'I will . . . we will!'

As she hurried off to post a letter for Uncle Jack, Kim mused that a lot of things in her life seemed to be changing suddenly. She'd lost her old job, and was working in a temporary one; Julie was becoming more independent every time she saw her; and now Nigel had found someone special. She and Julie would always be close, but university had widened her sister's horizons, and she'd made lots of friends, people Kim didn't know.

David Holland's interest in Julie still worried her a little. On top of all that, she was still confused about Alex Harrison, even though he never gave her special attention. There was something about him that drew her to him like a pin to a magnet. Battling her way back to the cottage against the wind, she decided it was time to think about her future more seriously. It was time to make a new start.

Uncle Jack's job meant he was always coming and going. Perhaps he'd retire in a couple of years' time. Kim presumed he'd covered the financial aspects of doing that, but at the moment he liked his work too much to settle down in the corner with books and the television. She ought to ask him if he'd thought about it in detail.

She'd probably have to find a job that was further away, and would either have to travel a longer distance or get a flat wherever she worked. She already knew there weren't many permanent jobs on offer locally, otherwise she wouldn't have ended up in her present one. She'd weigh up the pros and cons of buying a second-hand car for travelling to work, or finding a small flat and commuting back and forth to the cottage on weekends if Uncle Jack was home. She could probably use his old Jeep for a while if he was away on his next commission, but eventually she'd need her own car. Buying even a second-hand one would drain her savings completely.

She straightened her shoulders. It was also time to decide what she'd like to study. If she needed additional qualifications, she could work and go to evening classes. She could join a drama group, or a history club, and meet new people. The first thing to do was to find a new job. She'd only looked half-heartedly until now, but it was time to take things more seriously.

The following Sunday, she decided to visit the archaeological site again. She'd read an interesting article about it in the local midweek newspaper, and there were some accompanying pictures. Alex and Gloria were pictured outside the office, and there was a short summary of previous successful digs. The immediate area of the dig had been cordoned off, but so many interested visitors were turning up, they'd had to construct a viewing platform of scaffolding and wooden planking. Kim knew she could have asked if she could visit again to take another look, but she didn't want to contact Alex or Gloria. Alex had mentioned that they didn't welcome too many visitors on the site, and she for some reason she didn't want to see them together as any kind of twosome either. She cut the article out of the newspaper, folded Gloria out of sight, and put it in her bedside table.

After lunch, she asked Uncle Jack, 'Coming? I'm thinking of driving over to look at the excavation again. It might not be so busy at this time of day. Later on this afternoon, more people might turn up. The newspaper says they've constructed a viewing platform.'

'Yes, I read about it too.' He shook his head. 'I'm going to have forty winks.

Why don't you contact Alex, if you want to take another look? I'm sure he'd oblige, and let you have a much better view of everything.'

'I don't want to bother him. I'll see all I want to from the viewing platform. I can remember roughly what it looked like when he started, so I'll be able to see the difference. That's enough for me. I don't need an official guided tour again.'

'Please yourself. Will you be back for tea?'

'Probably long before then.'

'Good. Then enjoy yourself, love. I'll see you later.' He disappeared into the living room and Kim heard him making himself comfortable on the couch. She washed up, tidied her hair, grabbed her bag, and set off.

Gough's Burrow was a short drive from the centre of the village. It was a lovely afternoon and the roads were quiet. She passed fields where the cows and horses were poking about in the grass or standing under the trees along the borders. The Jeep purred along and she listened to the radio playing pop music. As she viewed the passing scenery out of the corner of her eye, she decided it was the loveliest time of the year. Most likely, people were still having lunch, or relaxing after it. Kim hoped that meant that there would be fewer casual visitors at the site. She was curious to see how much progress they'd made since last time.

It turned out that other people had had similar thoughts, and there were quite a few cars lined up neatly in the field. Kim wondered what the farmer thought about that. Perhaps he had some kind of agreement with Alex. The lane leading to the actual access was rutted and well-travelled. She walked to towards the visitors' platform. It was easy to find. It stuck out like a sore thumb in the surroundings. A notice warned visitors that they used the platform at their own risk. It was strategically placed, and gave people a good view of the dig. Kim could tell straight away there were several bigger sections on the site that were now under examination. She could see the remains of what were presumably Roman walls; helpers along their lengths were still busy excavating with their trowels, brushes, and buckets. No doubt the recent finds had fired imaginations and increased the number of volunteers.

'What are you doing here?'

She hadn't seen him approach, and his voice made her jump. She looked back and found him standing there. The colour flooded her cheeks for a moment. 'Hello, Alex!' she replied with deceptive calm and wondered why he always had this immediate quickening effect on her heartbeat. Explaining, she said, 'I wanted to see how far things were now. I thought it was a quiet time of day to visit, but . . . ' She looked around at the cluster of people along the edge of the scaffolding. ' . . . I see others have had the same idea.' She brushed some strands of wind-loosened hair off her face and decided to just enjoy his presence. She hadn't reckoned on seeing him, and that made it all the more stimulating. 'I didn't think you'd be here today. Do you never have a day off?'

'Not many, not when an excavation is on. I like to be around just in case someone does find something that's worth noting. I was just checking the bolts on the scaffolding, and looked up and saw you standing there.' He gave her a smile that sent her pulse racing out of control again. 'We're not legally responsible if something does happen — at least, I don't think we are — but I'd feel *morally* responsible if someone was injured. The council put it up for us, but they seem to forget that children seem to love jumping up and down as if it was a trampoline, or use it as a climbing frame. There are even idiots who could deliberately tamper with it and make it a safety risk.'

She nodded, and found she'd caught up and managed to steady her breath again. She wished she didn't feel like a teenager near her idol at a pop concert. She longed to reach out and touch him.

'I thought you might have come on another visit before this.' His eyes were brilliant blue in his face. He was slightly tanned, undoubtedly due to being outdoors so much.

She tried to sound nonchalant, but to her ears she still sounded slightly juvenile. 'I didn't want to disturb anyone, and keep you or Gloria from doing something more important.' She finished with a weak smile. 'Congratulations on the finds, by the way. We were all delighted when we heard. It must be very encouraging.'

He nodded and thrust his hands in his pocket. His expression steadied. 'I thought you just weren't interested when I heard nothing more from you.'

Her eyes widened. 'Did you? Whatever gave you that impression? The mere fact that I'm here now proves that I am.'

'Would you like a closer look?'

She shook her head and smiled. 'That's just what I wanted to avoid. It wouldn't be fair on the other visitors, would it? Perhaps you can show me around when you finally stop digging?'

His answering smile was lopsided and his eyes twinkled. 'I think you realize that the only time I ever stop digging is when the money runs out.'

'From what I hear, David is thinking about increasing his donation, isn't he?'

His smile faded. 'I wouldn't know. I'm not as close to him as you are.'

She looked puzzled. 'I'm not close to David. I haven't seen him since his flying visit a while ago. Even then, we talked more about my sister than about anything else.'

His voice was friendlier. 'You talked about your sister? I thought you and he were . . . '

She wondered why he'd put two and two together and made five. 'No! Why on earth should you think there was anything between us? I just wish I knew what he thinks about my sister. He has a bad reputation, and Julie is a lot younger. I'm afraid she'll end up overwhelmed by what he stands for and by all his money. I'm afraid she'll get hurt.' Kim didn't know why she was telling him, but it felt right because he was listening and looking sympathetic.

'How old is she?'

'Twenty-one soon.'

He shrugged. 'She's an adult. Kids grow up faster these days. Have you talked to her? Tried to find out if she's interested, and what she thinks?'

'No. I haven't had the chance for a chat recently. We don't see her very often any more. I don't want to play the heavy-handed big sister.'

He nodded. 'I think you shouldn't interfere. I'd guess that she knows too well what to expect from someone like David Holland. I think you have to let her make her own mistakes — if this is one! You shouldn't wrap her up in cotton wool. I expect you feel responsible because you are a little older and your parents are not around anymore.'

She nodded, and he continued, 'My advice, for what it's worth, is that you shouldn't pry. She's old enough to know what she's doing. I don't think David's ever been associated with drug abuse or that kind of thing. His lifestyle is a result of the fact he's rich. There's nothing wrong with that. Personally, I find him likeable because he's generally very honest. You know where you stand when you talk to him. I wonder how much of what we read in the newspapers about him is actually true.'

'I hope that at least three-quarters is wrong!'

'If it helps, I must say the more I talk to him, the better I like him. He's single-minded, he's very intelligent, and he doesn't stand fools gladly; but he needs to be objective, being in charge of the kind of financial empire he owns. In many ways I can empathise with him. I don't suffer fools gladly either, and as far as my work is concerned I'm very single-minded too.'

He changed the subject and pointed

towards the site. 'Right over on the other side of the site is where they discovered the tablet telling us when the Romans were here. From the position of that lucky find, we can work out where the other gates might have been. I'm hoping we'll find the other tablets. The fort's headquarters building was in the middle. Usually it faced an arched doorway in the centre of the front wall. All administration tasks were handled there. Generally, in legionary fortresses, the headquarters was divided into three sections: a colonnaded courtyard, an inner covered assembly hall, and perhaps a couple of small rooms at the back . . . ' He stopped suddenly and looked at her ruefully. 'I'm sorry! When I get going, there's no stopping me. I just wanted to divert your thoughts away from David and your sister.'

She laughed. 'That's okay, I don't mind. I shouldn't bore you with my problems. The dig is very interesting, and it's great to see a kind of outline of where things used to be. I never imagined I would ever get this close to an excavation site, and I know next to nothing about what a Roman fort would have looked like, either. Your explanations are very welcome. I think people like me tend to imagine that Roman buildings and Roman behaviour were romantic, but I expect they weren't.'

'But they were way ahead of other civilizations of their time. When you think about their bathhouses, the way they organized their armies, the roads and buildings they constructed ... quite remarkable achievements. Imagine being able to have a hot bath in the middle of winter in a place like this!'

She laughed, and his eyes twinkled. 'It must definitely have been sheer heaven!' she agreed. 'But they could only uphold their power by having slaves.'

His mouth twitched in amusement. 'True! But you have to conquer a land before you can enslave the population, and to do that you need a well-organized army.' He looked at his watch. 'Would you like to look at some of the finds?'

Her brows lifted. 'Do you still have them here?'

He nodded. 'Usually, all metal work and any special finds are immediately removed from site for security reasons, but Mr Booth asked us to delay sending them away until he's contacted David and found out if he wants to take a look before we finally dispatch them.'

He held out his hand and she took it. Kim felt the strength of his long fingers and an intensive sensation of physical wellbeing during the brief seconds they were united. Once she was on solid ground, he freed her, and they walked alongside each other towards the office.

'Is Gloria working today?' Kim couldn't help asking.

She felt relief when he said, 'No, she's gone up to London with some pictures and a couple of Saxon coins to get some advice from a colleague about them. I think it is always best to ask an expert. I'm pretty solid on Roman remains, but I don't see why someone with more knowledge about other areas shouldn't give us the benefit of his brain if we need it.'

They reached the container office, and he opened the door with a bunch of keys from his pocket. He went straight to a low metal cupboard in the corner. He unlocked it and came back with some clear plastic bags containing the things he wanted to show her.

'These are fairly fresh finds, straight from one of the trenches, but they're still very recognizable.'

Kim studied the coins inside one of the bags he put on the table. They were still splattered with mud. A second bag contained something that looked like a long pin with a large head, and another some beads. She felt obliged to comment.

'Amazing to imagine someone last handled them almost two thousand years ago. How do you remember exactly where they were found?'

'Each bag contains two waterproof labels, with the site code and the context number of the deposit from which they were unearthed. These labels are kept with the finds all the way through their processing, and mean that, when they are analysed, the information can be related straight back to the feature on site that they came from.'

'Do the beads mean there were women in the fort? Or do you think they were booty or intended as presents?'

He shrugged. 'Your guess is as good as mine. Perhaps some officers did have their families with them, or had relationships with local women. That long pin is definitely a hair decoration, so women certainly lived here. Forts were customarily male-dominated places. Would you like a cup of coffee?'

'No thanks, I promised Uncle Jack I'd be back by teatime. Thank you for showing me the finds. I feel quite privileged!'

Playfully, he commented, 'If you ask me nicely, I'd like to come back and have tea with you both.'

She was lost for words for a moment. 'I'm afraid haven't anything special for tea today. In fact, I think there are only biscuits and some stale fruitcake.'

'Sounds good to me. You don't live very far from here. I've earned a break, and it's sometimes good to get away for a while. I'll just tell the woman in charge today that she can reach me by phone in an emergency. You can go ahead and I'll catch up with you.'

She nodded. She felt slightly bowled over by the situation. A short time ago, she'd been sure he wanted to ignore her — and now he was going out of his way to be informative and inviting himself to tea!

She left him locking the finds back into the cupboard. She hurried back to the Jeep and set off. If she was quick, she could call at the supermarket on the way, and get some fresh cakes . . . but a glance at her watch told her they'd be closed by the time she got there. Her heart was in her mouth, and she felt silly enough to look forward immensely to having him in the cottage for a time.

She found Uncle Jack still stretched out on the couch, with a newspaper over his face and snoring gently. She left him for a moment and hurried to the kitchen. Preparing a tray with the tea things, she wished she had a frozen cake in the deep freezer. She shrugged. She had warned him she had nothing to offer, and he hadn't seemed to mind.

The sound of rattling china woke her uncle up. He ran his hand over his face, reached for his glasses from the table, and lowered his legs to search for his slippers. 'Back already? What's the time?'

'Gone four. Alex is coming.'

'Alex? What for?'

Kim replied, while arranging the cups and saucers, 'No special reason. He more or less invited himself to tea. I warned him there was no fresh cake. He said it didn't matter. He showed me some of the finds from the site. It was interesting. I expect he wants to tell you about their progress.'

He looked at her speculatively and nodded. 'I quite like the chap. What do you think of him?'

Kim coloured. 'Me?'

'Yes, you! Nothing flusters you normally, but I can tell you are in a tizzy at the moment. It can only have something to do with Alex.' He grinned.

'Don't be silly! He's a world authority on Roman history. Why should I be interested in him in a personal way? Our lifestyles are miles apart.'

'That's a lot of balderdash! What has work got to do with what you think about someone? You *are* interested in him, aren't you?'

Kim was saved from answering because the doorbell rang.

They spent a pleasant hour together. Alex even ate a piece of the dry fruitcake and said it was just fine. Uncle Jack fished around for reasons to leave them alone, but Kim managed to thwart his attempts. She felt embarrassed when she thought that he was trying to push them together. If Alex noticed anything, he didn't comment.

Alex told Uncle Jack about the dig, asked him about his forthcoming trip to Venezuela, and mentioned that David Holland might visit the site soon. Time passed quickly. Kim used the opportunity to study Alex more carefully. She liked the way he relaxed and gave her the feeling he was happy in their company.

Kim liked the way he looked, too. She liked his expressive face, she liked the slightly humorous way he described the dig, and she liked his voice. She liked him full stop. She liked him more than was good for her peace of mind. Why would someone like him be interested in someone like her? His education, his professional standing, and his background were totally different to hers. Her colour was heightened when she went with him to the door to see him off.

'Thanks for the tea. Just what I needed.'

'You're welcome. I wish I could have offered you a decent tea, and not the hotchpotch you got!'

His eyes twinkled, and there was something else hidden in their depths. 'It was perfect. I'll invite you to tea one day. We could share a tea with all the trimmings. There's a nice little teashop not far from here in Under Lockley.'

She was flustered. 'Yes, I know it.'

'Good! We'll arrange something. I have to watch my schedule, but as soon as I've checked it I'll be in touch. I'd like to settle something now, but I must keep to the rules and watch my step when the excavation is in progress! I'm responsible for it, and if I keep flitting off for private reasons, things could go wrong.'

He turned away without waiting for a comment, and lifted his hand once he was seated in his car. He reversed down the short driveway, and then disappeared from sight.

Kim shut the door and felt like whooping. She skipped upstairs to be alone and enjoy the sensation before she had to face Uncle Jack again.

A couple of minutes later, she felt calmer and more in control. It wasn't a real date, but it was the next best thing; and she was growing to like him so much that even an invitation to tea in a country teashop could set her pulse hurtling upwards.

10

The next day, back at work, Derek passed on the information that David was coming again. He'd juggled his appointments to make enough free time in his schedule.

Kim kept herself busy doing some typing for one of the department heads and tried to put Alex out of her mind. She hoped that his invitation to tea was a real possibility and not just a polite promise. On Tuesday morning, her heart was in her mouth when she picked up the telephone and heard his voice.

'Hi! How about tomorrow afternoon for going to that teashop? Once the morning excavations are finished, everyone begins to flag, and things quieten down. I'd look forward to tea with you at that place, if you have time.' He paused. 'I didn't think afternoon tea would be your uncle's thing, that's why I only asked you.'

She tried not to sound overenthusiastic. 'You're right, I'm almost sure he wouldn't come. Tomorrow is fine by me. Shall we meet there? It's about half-way between your dig and this office.'

'Good! See you tomorrow, then. Three o'clock?' Papers were rustling in the background, so either he was talking while doing something else, or Gloria was in the room.

'Yes — till tomorrow!' Kim could hardly wait to see him, and told herself not to be silly. It was only his way of paying back some hospitality. Shared tea in a teashop, mid-afternoon, was definitely not a romantic rendezvous.

That evening, Julie phoned them. After the usual questions and answers, Kim said, 'David Holland mentioned he was getting in touch with you, to ask you out for a meal. Did he call?'

There was a momentary pause. 'Yes, he did. It was a really nice evening.

He's not like the newspaper reports make him out to be. I was going to mention it to you, but you've beaten me to it. I was surprised, but pleasantly so.'

Kim thought about Alex's words. Julie was old enough to judge and make her own decisions. She couldn't help asking, 'Do you think you'll see him again?'

'Yes, I do. He said next time he came to visit the excavation site, he'd be in touch, and he asked if we could meet again — if I had the time.'

'You will be sensible, love, won't you? Don't let the money and all the rest make you blind to the real person behind all of that.'

Sounding quite exasperated, Julie said, 'Kim, I'm not a baby. I realize David is someone who is very different from me. It doesn't mean I can't like him, and it doesn't mean I can't give him the chance to be himself when we're together. You know very well that money and power don't mean a thing to me. I think he realizes that by now, too. I've always been very honest with him. I don't act any differently with him than I do with anyone else. Perhaps he'll get bored with me fast and I'll never see him again. Perhaps he'll find he needs people around him who constantly flatter his ego. I couldn't maintain an act just to keep him interested in me. I am what I am; and he's David Holland.'

'That's okay, then. I just wanted to be sure. After all, he is an outstanding personality.'

'Yes: he's attention-grabbing, he's very intelligent, and he's out of the ordinary. He's also cultivated and very well-mannered, and a lot of fun to be with. He's very interested in me and what I'm doing with mathematics. In fact, he is quite unique.'

Kim was reassured. It sounded like Julie understood the pros and cons.

Next morning she dressed in a favourite outfit of hers, a sea-green trouser suit which emphasised her neat waist and slim hips. She wouldn't have time to come home to change if she were to get to the tearoom on time. She'd cleared with Derek that she was entitled to a few hours off, even though she was only a temporary employee. She felt a bit like a teenager looking forward to her first date with someone she'd fancied for too long.

Freshening her make-up before she set off, she was glad she'd borrowed the Jeep. The weather was miserable and there were constant heavy showers. The windscreen wipers worked in a fast rhythm as they tried to restore a clear view. The rain battered the glass in transparent strips and dots.

Shaking the residue of rain from her umbrella when she entered the tearoom, she found it was almost empty. Two women were in one of the corners, surrounded by bulging plastic bags. They'd finished their tea some time ago, but the rain didn't encourage them to leave, and they were busy gossiping. Alex wasn't there, so Kim chose a table near the window. The room's decoration was comfortable and rustic. The ancient black beams were low, and the tables were covered with pale green tablecloths. A single rose in a glass vase provided the right kind of atmosphere, and helped banished the feeling of café-functionality.

The waitress came, and Kim explained she was waiting for someone. Time seemed to drag as she sat and watched through the window the people hurrying by. She checked her watch constantly. In the end, she felt too embarrassed to just sit and stare, so she ordered a pot of tea and went on waiting. She wondered what had happened. She didn't think that he was the kind of person who just wouldn't turn up. Did he have her telephone number? She fumbled in her bag for her phone and checked her incoming calls. There was nothing. She had his office number, but decided it was childish to phone him to demand an explanation.

One hour and an empty teapot later,

she admitted that that hope was finally gone. No doubt there was a reason why he hadn't come, but her disappointment was too great for her to feel anything but disillusioned. She put on her coat, paid the waitress, left the empty café, and went out into the rain again. She was glad to reach the Jeep and slide onto the old leather seat. She struggled to fit the seat-belt tongue into the slot because she was concentrating on keeping control of the looming tears at the back of her eyes.

She was being so childish, but she couldn't help herself. It had only been an invitation to share afternoon tea in a tearoom, and something must have delayed him. She managed to pull herself together again once she'd blown her nose and straightened her back. On the journey home, she was almost glad that the rain was still heavy and came down in sheets. It meant she had to concentrate harder on driving more carefully than usual. She parked in front of the cottage and remained sitting where she was for a moment before she turned off the engine. She felt she had herself under control by the time she made a dash for the front door.

Shaking the rain off her jacket and depositing her umbrella in the stand, she went in search of her Uncle. He looked up when she came in.

'There you are. Awful weather, isn't it? It's bucketing down, and no sign of it clearing up. Shall I make us a cup of tea?'

'No, I'll do it.' She was glad to have something to do.

She was on her way to the kitchen when his voice stopped her in her tracks. 'Oh! Before I forget — Alex phoned. He said he didn't have your number. He told me to tell you that they'd had a break-in at the site, and he couldn't get away. I didn't realize you were meant to be meeting him.'

'A break-in? You mean a robbery?'

'Yes. Apparently someone has taken some of the finds from a steel cabinet they had in the corner of the office. The door wasn't damaged in any way, so they presume it was an insider.'

A weight lifted inside. There was a genuine reason why he hadn't come. 'Gosh! I wonder how many people have keys. Alex showed me a couple of things when I was there on Sunday.'

'Did he? They can't understand how someone managed to steal anything without damaging the cupboard. Some-one must have used a key. Alex has one, of course, and his assistant has one, but someone else must have made a copy. After he or she took what they wanted, they even locked the cabinet again.'

'And why would a thief do that? Have they taken everything?'

'No, that's what's so strange. They've only taken a couple of items. Some coins, some necklace beads, and some-thing else. There were a lot of other items in there: some of them were a lot more interesting, but they left them alone.' He rustled his newspaper and adjusted his reading glasses. 'Alex said he'd be in touch later.'

Kim nodded. 'I expect he's frustrated and angry. He feels very responsible for everything. I remember him mentioning that normally the items would have been sent to be officially registered, but they'd hung on to them because David wanted to see them.'

'The whole business seems strange to me. I know that a lot of treasure hunters would love Roman or Saxon finds . . . but who knew they were in that cabinet in the corner of the office? I expect they'll want to interview anyone who knew it was there.'

'I'll get the tea.' In the kitchen, she had time to think about Alex's dilemma. She could imagine how he felt. He'd shown her a couple of the finds just a day or two ago. He was justifiably proud that the dig was successful, and had confirmed his hypothesis that Gough's Burrow had been a Roman — and, later, a Saxon — habitation. Would the police want to talk to her too?

The more she thought about it, the more she wanted to phone and sympathise. His phone rang several times before she heard his voice.

'Harrison!'

'Alex? This is Kim. I'm sorry to hear about what happened.'

There was a moment's silence. 'Yes, so am I, of course. I'm sorry about this afternoon too, but I had no way to contact you. I don't have your private number.'

'That's okay. Don't worry. You have enough on your plate at present. I don't want to bother you, I just wanted you to know I'm sorry.'

'The police have just left. There was a team here checking for fingerprints.'

'Any chance of them finding the culprit?'

'No, I don't think so. If your house gets burgled and prized possessions disappear, it's clearly quite another kettle of fish. Our things are just a couple of ancient artefacts. They promised to do their best.' His voice was more indulgent in its tone when he said, 'Look, do you have time to meet me? I'd like to go for a walk somewhere to clear my head. After all of this, I feel very irritated. Everyone I talk to makes suggestions and sympathetic comments.'

'That's perfectly natural under the circumstances, isn't it?' The knowledge that he wanted her company sent a feeling of warmth through her. 'Yes, let's meet! What about the Forest Walk? It's rained all day, but the main tracks are well-drained.' She looked out of the window. 'It's stopped raining, but I don't think many people will go there anymore at this time of day. Do you know where it is?'

'Yes, I've been there before. A good idea! I'll meet you in a quarter of an hour. If you get there before me, wait in the car park.'

'Will do!' Kim was barely able to control her excitement. She grabbed the car keys and a dry anorak from the hallstand. Popping her head round the sitting room door, she saw Uncle Jack was watching the TV and sipping his tea. 'I'm going out for a while. Be back soon!'

He lifted his hand in acknowledgement without answering.

The sky was still full of racing clouds, but the rain had stopped. She drove through the village and past the flat fields with their thick bordering hedges. She was impatient to get there. As she neared their meeting point the roads narrowed and from there on they were in bad repair. She rounded the last bend and pulled up onto the grass verge. She felt a wave of pleasure when she saw Alex was already waiting. He looked tall and powerful, standing beneath a group of birches with delicate boughs and shifting leaves. She stared wordlessly across at him for a second or two, her heart pounding as she admitted silently to herself that she loved him in a way she didn't think possible. He moved towards her and she hurried to get out. She was still thinking that she loved him, and she had to swallow hard before she managed a smile.

They faced each other for a moment before he said, 'Shall we stick to the main path? There's no point in going elsewhere, the ground is soaked through.'

He stuck his hands in his leather jacket and viewed her as she nodded. Side by side, they left the car park and started up the path with its gradual climb. The trees bordering the footpath cut off the wind, and the air was fresh and cool with the scent of pine.

Kim said, 'Do you want me to ignore the topic of the theft? We can talk about something else if you like.'

He ran his hand through his hair and gave her a faint smile. 'No, it's alright. It's different when *you* want to talk about it. You're not so involved. The people on site are, and they tend to be too wrapped up in exaggerated worry. As if it was a personal loss.'

'Well, it is in a sense, isn't it?

186

Everyone has worked so hard to find something, and then someone comes along and pinches it for some foul reason of their own. I gathered the police have come and gone?'

He lessened his long strides when he noticed she had to accelerate to keep in step. 'Yes. I don't think they can do much to solve the mystery, but an inquiry must follow official procedures.'

'It's awful. Especially since you were holding onto the items because of David. I presume that normally you would have sent them to be officially registered by now? You mentioned that when I was there. Uncle Jack said they only took one or two things.'

He shoved his hands deeper into his pockets and stared ahead. 'That's the funny thing about it all. I expect they'll end up on the black market.'

'But surely people would be reluctant to buy something if they didn't know where it came from?'

He ripped the words out impatiently: 'Most of the people who are interested in buying such things couldn't care less where they came from. If the price is right and it's special, they'll take it.'

'You took photos?'

He ran his hand through his hair and came to a sudden halt. There was a fork in the track ahead of them. The paths continued to climb in two shallow curves bordered by thick pines. 'Yes, of course, but that doesn't help much.'

'Why are they special?'

'Apparently, the coins are quite rare, so they'll fetch a decent price. The other things aren't so valuable historically. Similar ones are found often all over the Roman Empire, but a collector would still love to own them.'

'Did many people know they were there?'

He shrugged. 'That's what's so strange. I knew, Gloria knew; but people on the site probably believed we followed the normal procedure and they were already elsewhere. No one keeps important finds on site too long.' He paused. 'And, of course, you knew, because I showed them to you that day.'

She stared wordlessly across at him and her heart pounded wildly. She nodded without thinking. Studying her face for a moment, he suddenly leaned forward, took hold of her shoulders, and kissed her. What she felt had nothing to do with reason. Subconsciously, she was aware of the rustling of the wind in the trees . . . and his face, so close and so full of silent expectation. There was a tingling in her stomach. Instinctively, she returned his kiss, and it set alight a flicker of answering emotion in his intense eyes. She was fully aware of his body brushing against hers, and she felt pure delight when his arms enfolded her and he kissed her again.

This time it was slow and thoughtful. Her lips were still warm and moist from his when he held her at arms' length and said, 'I've wanted to do that for a while.'

She managed to find her voice and said, 'Have you?'

'Before I forget, I should tell you. The police will want to talk to you.'

Kim didn't manage to adjust fast enough from the delight of his kisses to such sensible words. She stared at him in silence. She still wanted something more personal. Words about them, words about what had just happened. Was she placing too much significance on a few kisses? She tried to work out precisely how she felt, and how she should react.

In dazed exasperation, she asked, 'What do you mean, the police want to talk to me? Just to confirm I was there, and that you showed me the finds?'

His jaw clenched and he nodded. 'They'll want to know exactly where you were on Sunday afternoon, and whatever you've done since then.'

'Pardon?' She stiffened under his hands and automatically stepped back, out of his protection. Her eyes were wide and the words almost stuck in her throat. 'Just a minute! Am I under suspicion?'

Frowning, he answered, 'Don't worry. I expect it's just routine. They have to check every possibility.'

She swallowed hard, trying not to show her anger. 'You don't think I'm a thief, I hope? What on earth would I do with finds from a historical site?'

He shrugged. 'Kim, you'd be surprised at how easily people are tempted, and how simple it is for anyone to sell such things. There's a market, and there are always ways and means. Anyone can find an interested buyer quite quickly. If you're clever and know how to use the Internet, a bogus contact email address in an Internet café is all you need. No one remembers who it was later.'

She could have listened to anyone else saying such things, but not Alex. The colour left her face. Was he implying that she might have done it? Was he so suspicious that he had asked her here to give her the chance to confess and return the stolen items? She felt ice spreading through her stomach and her temper rising. 'Is that why you kissed me just now? To soften the blow?'

'Blow? What blow? I'm only telling you the police want to talk to you.'

She searched in vain for signs of understanding about how she must feel.

Noticing her expression, he rushed to utter, 'Don't be silly, Kim. No one is accusing you of anything. Even if we are still getting to know each other, I don't believe you would ever do such a thing — but you have to understand too that after today nothing would surprise me. Someone I know and trusted did it. You are involved because you are one of the last people who saw the items. I'm leaving it up to the police to sort things out, and so should you. There's no reason for you to feel concerned about a few questions.'

The colour left her face. All Kim could think was that he didn't have enough faith in her to reject the possibility outright. Trying to hide the hurt, her voice was cold. 'That's fine, then! The police can find me at home or at work. No doubt you've already told them where.' She couldn't think straight or stay any longer. She couldn't imagine why he'd even wanted to meet her in the first place if she was still on his list of suspects. It hurt to think he could doubt her honesty. She turned to go.

Alex was thunderstruck by her reaction. He knew he should have phrased things better, but he was still too uncertain of how she felt about him. He should have realized she would pick up the wrong indication . . . and she should have realized he always spoke with complete honesty. He lifted his hand in a motion of restraint. 'Kim, don't be silly. I'm not accusing you of anything.'

She ignored the gesture and started off back down the path. Over her shoulder, she said, 'That's not the signal I'm getting. You don't trust me, Alex, otherwise you wouldn't tell me how easy it is to dispose of stolen goods one minute, and that we don't know each other very well the next. How right you are!' She hurried on, not waiting for his reply.

Alex stood and watched her in bewilderment. He'd just made general comments, not accusations. By the time alarm set in, she was already halfway down the track. He knew he had to put it right and began to follow her. She was already too far ahead and then she began to run. By the time she reached the Jeep, she heard him coming, but she was already belted in and driving away by the time he reached the car park.

★   ★   ★

In the rear-view mirror, she could still see the look of surprise and annoyance on his face. Kim felt humiliated and miserable. She'd felt ecstatic when he kissed her, but his words had brought her back to earth with a thud. Tears gathered at the back of her eyes and she let them flow. She didn't understand why he'd bothered to kiss her. One thing was certain: he didn't feel for her in the way she did for him.

She didn't drive to the cottage directly. She took a side road and pulled onto the verge. She needed time to order her jumbled thoughts before she went home. She wished Julie were there.

If Uncle Jack noticed she was quieter than usual that evening, he didn't comment. Alex didn't phone back either, and she took that to be another sign that he didn't care, She decided to talk to Julie. They'd always helped with each other's problems. Julie would listen and make sensible comments.

Her uncle settled in front of the television after supper to watch a documentary about Australia. Normally, she would have joined him, but she had more important things to do this evening. There was a telephone extension in the main bedroom, and she dialled Julie's mobile number.

'Hi there! I've been wondering how

things were at home. I intended phoning tomorrow.'

'Everything is fine . . . but I'm not.'

Her sister's voice heightened. 'You're not? Why?'

Kim explained as best she could. Julie was silent for a moment, then she said, 'It sounds like you're in love with him. Are you?'

'I must be. I've never felt like this about anyone before.'

She heard Julie chuckling.

'We don't even know each other properly. He's a professor, and quite famous in his chosen field. I'm Miss Nobody.'

'That's a stupid comment. What is love? Who can define it? Fate gives us a chance. If you listen to your heart and fall in love, it doesn't matter who the other person is, or what they do. Love is blind!'

Sitting on the edge of the bed, Kim noticed mindlessly that the window was open. The sun had almost disappeared, and the chilly winds were fretting at the hangings. She nodded, unseen by Julie on the other end of the connection. 'I suppose you're right, but I wish I'd never met him now.'

'You know that isn't true, so stop lying. The mere fact that you phoned me and told me about him shows me just how much you care. Know something? From the sound of it, this is a storm in a teacup. He didn't accuse you of stealing anything, did he? He just talked about how easy it was to get rid of stolen items, and that the police have to do their job. I think it's up to you now to get in touch with him and admit you overreacted. Otherwise he'll believe you're just neurotic.'

'I can't face him after I acted like that.'

'Rubbish! If you don't, he'll think you intend to ignore him. This isn't the Middle Ages when men make all the decisions. What about an email? That's neutral territory.'

Reluctantly, Kim promised, 'I'll think about it.'

'Do, and I'll find out if David knows anything about the police investigation.'

'David? Are you that close? Are you seeing him?'

There was a moment of silence. 'People walk into your life one day, and you have a special feeling about them. It's as though as if you've been waiting all your life for them. That's what I felt when I met David for the first time. And I think that's what you feel about Alex.'

'And David . . . does he feels the same about you?'

'Yes, I'm certain that he does.'

Kim was startled by her sister's words. 'Don't let him hurt you.'

'Know something? I don't think he will. I don't think he ever will. He's very protective and says he loves me. That's quite wonderful. He wants me to finish my degree whatever happens, and we won't rush into anything. The press hasn't caught on to us yet and he's trying to keep it that way so that we can spend some ordinary time together.'

'How often have you met him?'

'As often as he can make time for us to be together. I'm so glad I've told you; it means I can bring him home one weekend to meet Uncle Jack and Linda.'

Kim's mind boggled at the idea of them entertaining someone who was used to living off champagne and caviar, but Julie sounded quite serious. She liked David too, but she didn't want Julie to end up with a broken heart — only time would tell.

Julie's voice brought her back to earth again. 'Anyway, enough about me. Send your Alex an email, and tell him you overreacted and took things too personally.'

'I'll think about it. I'm glad we've talked. It has helped . . . and perhaps I did act stupidly. If you care about someone, you do stupid things some-times.'

Julie laughed softly on the other end of the line. 'How right you are. Don't lose any sleep, love. Send him a nice message and wait and see how he reacts. Let me know what happens.'

'I will.' Kim was tempted to add greetings for David, but it was too early to play the loving sister-in-law yet. 'Bye!'

After spending a sleepless night, she took time next morning in sending him an email stating she'd acted stupidly. She didn't want to sound as if she was begging, but she wanted him to see that she realized she'd overreacted. In the end, she felt happy with the resulting short text, and after a moment of hesitation she pressed the Send button. She only had his office email address, so she'd kept the wording neutral in case Gloria saw it.

Later that day, after Kim feeling as if she'd been sitting on hot coals waiting for a response, Derek mentioned that Alex had been suddenly called away yesterday evening to a site he'd been in charge of in the North of England. They needed him to corroborate the authenticity of some new finds they'd made.

'He'll be gone for a couple of days.'

'What about the investigation into the theft?'

Derek looked thoughtful. 'Apparently that is still going on. It looks like they don't have much hope of ever finding the stolen items. Alex gave them photos and descriptions, of course, but it's not as important as if national treasures had been stolen! David Holland has been in touch with Mr Booth this morning, and said he'd put his security firm on to double-checking things. The police probably won't like a private firm sticking its nose in, but Mr Booth tried to calm the waves by explaining to the officer in charge that Holland is providing the money for the dig and that he has a special interest in finding out what happened. Whatever the police think, they can't stop Holland's people making their own inquiries.'

'The more the merrier! The police will want to interview me, I expect. They haven't been in touch up to now.'

'Yes, we heard you visited the site on

Sunday and that Alex showed you some of the finds. You are probably the last uninvolved person who saw the items before they were stolen.'

Kim felt good to hear that 'uninvolved'. Derek had immediately assumed that to be the case. If Alex had used similar expressions, and if she hadn't been so touchy, things might have ended quite differently that day. Why had she gone off the rails? Had she been over-emotional because of their kisses? 'Yes; I only saw a couple of items. Alex didn't take everything out of the safe to show me, just the finds he probably thought I'd recognize easily. Do you think I ought to contact the police?'

He shook his head. 'I expect they know where to find you. Alex will have told them you visited the site. They'll either contact you, or ask you to call in to a local station and give a statement.'

That was exactly what happened. Kim called at the local police station, and a young officer took her statement. Once she'd finished, Kim couldn't help asking, 'Is there any progress?'

'Not as far as I know. Your statement concurs completely with Mr Harrison's account. We just have to wait and see what the rest of the investigation brings to light.'

Julie rang her that evening. 'I had to find out if you sent that email.'

'Yes, but he hasn't seen it yet. He had to go to another excavation near the Scottish border, so he won't get it until his return.'

'Oh, pity! Still, he'll get it eventually. And David told me he's put his people on to the investigation.'

'So I heard. I can't imagine that they'll find anything, if the police can't make any progress.'

'David said they're first-class. He probably pays them top wages. His privacy, and that of his family, is one of the most important aspects of his life. Have you thought about phoning Alex?'

'No, I won't do that; at least, not until I know he's back.'

'Well, when he is, if you don't get a

reply to your email within a day or two, promise me that you'll phone him?'

Kim's voice wavered. 'Speaking to him will be even harder. It'll look like I'm chasing him.'

'And what if it does? Do you want to put things right, or not?'

'Yes, I suppose so!'

Julie laughed. 'All is fair in love and war. He must be quite a special man if you feel so strongly about him.'

'He is, and I do.'

A couple of days passed. There was no news from the police. However, Julie sent her a text to say that David's people were on to something . . . but that it was too early to go into detail about it.

At the end of the following week, Kim heard that Alex was back again. She waited anxiously all day for him to respond to her email. Nothing happened. At first, she put it down to the fact that he might be extremely busy, catching up with urgent work and decision-making on site. When the clock showed it was time for her to finish for the day, her hopes faded. She was reluctant to even think about phoning him, but she'd promised Julie, and so she plucked up all her courage and dialled the number.

'Gloria Thurston!'

With her heart still in her mouth, she came back to earth and said, 'Oh, Gloria. I wanted to speak to Alex. Is he there?'

'No, I'm sorry but he's not. He's outside looking at some wall they've started to uncover. Is it something important? If it is, I'll get him.'

'No . . . no, nothing that can't wait. Will you tell him that I called, please, and that I'd like him to phone back when he's free? I'm finishing work now, but he knows our home number.'

'Yes, of course. I'll be sure to give him your message. Bye, Kim!'

'Bye!'

She hurried home, hoping Alex wouldn't phone the minute she left the office. After greeting her uncle as usual, she managed to ask quite casually, 'Any calls?'

'No, expecting one?'

'No, not really.'

He nodded. Kim was glad he knew nothing about how she really felt about Alex. It would be embarrassing. She turned towards the kitchen. 'I'll get us some tea. Hungry?'

'No, but a cup of tea would be just the thing.'

Kim waited and waited all evening. There was no return call from Alex. All the pleasure went out of the day. She automatically made them spaghetti Bolognese, and ate despite having no appetite, just to thwart Uncle Jack's curiosity.

When her uncle left for the sitting room again, she could let her emotions freewheel, and felt only an all-encompassing dismay. She didn't expect Alex to be overjoyed to hear from her after she'd run off and left him like that, but she felt she knew him well enough to know he wasn't unfair by nature — surely he wouldn't ignore her like this unless he felt embarrassed and didn't know how to react?

The knowledge that he had ignored her email, and her phone call made her despondent and miserable. She could even imagine how his face would look — a dark expression and his mouth set in a hard line whenever he heard her name. She tried to tell herself it didn't matter. They'd never been more than acquaintances, and his kisses were merely slip-ups. Why would someone like him have the slightest interest in someone like her?

It was too early to do what she longed to — hide away with her misery in her room. She stuffed her feet into her wellingtons, standing next to the kitchen door. Grabbing the rake and clippers, she hurried into the garden and took her revenge on an unsuspecting privet hedge. As she worked, she told herself she'd been a fool.

Her uncle was making himself a cup of cocoa when she came in. The kitchen was full of shadows, and he chatted about the programme he'd been watching and the news of the day. Kim spent longer than necessary removing her wellingtons, and then kept her back to him as she cleaned them over the rubbish bin. She didn't want him to see her face. He would notice her red eyes and ask her what was wrong. He wished her goodnight, and picking a book up from the table, said he was having an early night for once.

Kim stood looking out of the window at the ancient apple tree with bark that was gnarled and thick. It had seen a lot of comings and goings. Looking at the western sky, she saw it was now drained of colour, and there was only one bright star swimming in a sea of black velvet. She fought hard against the tears at the back of her eyes again, and her determination faltered. She told herself she'd merely imagined she loved Alex. She checked the answering machine, checked her phone, but there was nothing. She hadn't felt so unhappy and totally lost since she was twelve and at her parents' funeral.

But she'd survived that, and she'd survive this too. It was time to pull herself together and get on with her life. She had to learn to forget Alex Harrison.

She tried to tell herself that it had been merely infatuation, and she'd been carried away by the fame and the aura that surrounded him. They were bound to meet again before she left for another job because of the excavation work . . . but perhaps she needed that. She needed to see him and know that he felt nothing for her. She'd then be able to put all ghosts aside and get on with her life again.

She didn't sleep much, and Derek asked if she was ill the next day, because she was so pale.

For a couple of days, work went on as usual. She concentrated on keeping the sponsored accounts up to date, and helping with typing for Derek or anyone else he was responsible for. She finally decided to fill in the forms to study history and languages with the Open University, and send them off. She forgot her idea of buying her own car, and earmarked the rest of her savings to cover the cost of the rest of the course. She wasn't yet sure what she'd do when she had a degree. Did she have the qualities needed to be a good teacher? Perhaps she could go abroad and use a degree and her work experience in an interesting job? It was also time for her to start studying the situations vacant advertisements in the paper and at the job centre. She didn't know how much longer the excavation work would continue, but if she was lucky enough to get a new job soon, perhaps Derek or one of his students could finish things off for her.

She was making coffee when the door flew open, and was caught off-guard when she saw Alex standing there. He stood immobile for a moment, and their eyes met.

She stared wordlessly across the

room at him, her heart pounding out of control. She pulled herself together and struggled to maintain an even, conciliatory tone. Her colour heightened when she uttered the words, 'Morning, Alex! Can I help you?'

The beginnings of a smile faded as he stared at her. There was a long silence. He had expected another reaction, and he was now unsure and baffled. Whatever his intention had been, he wavered and considered the situation very carefully before he closed the door and came across. He retained his affability outwardly, but his lips were formed in a stiff smile. His eyes hardened and his voice was full of cool undertones. 'Morning!'

'Back again? I heard you were needed elsewhere?' Her voice sounded shakier than she would have liked, but it was all she could manage.

'Yes.' His gaze was direct and concerting. 'It's always good to know one is needed, isn't it?'

If he was fencing with words, Kim

didn't know how to counter them on the spur of the moment. She was annoyed with herself when she noticed her hands were shaking, and she made haste to grab a mug of coffee and hold it tightly. Her feelings for him weren't logical, and all her well-meant intentions of forgetting him went up in smoke. Much to her dismay, she found the pull was stronger now than it had ever been. Nothing she could do would stop her loving him, and she would never forget him either.

His blue eyes narrowed and hardened. He reached into an inner pocket and handed her the recorder. 'It's full again.'

She nodded, and muttered hastily, 'No problem! Good.' She plonked her mug on a nearby filing cabinet and took the replacement out of the desk drawer. They exchanged machines.

He pocketed the Dictaphone and turned to go. His voice, though quiet, had an ominous quality. 'I'll make sure you get the recorder on time, but I won't bother you with my presence any more. I can take a hint!' He exited before she had time to react.

Kim sat down heavily in the nearest chair, and wondered if she'd dreamed what had just happened.

She didn't mention that she'd seen Alex again when she spoke to Julie the following evening. She couldn't face repeating everything, and she hedged around the subject. She hoped that once she'd got used to the fact that Alex had decided to avoid her, she'd be strong enough to talk to Julie about it.

Julie was bursting with other news. 'Guess who they think stole those things?'

'Who?'

'Gloria Thurston. She's Alex's assistant, isn't she?'

'Gloria!' Kim couldn't believe it. 'Good heavens! She's the last person I'd suspect. Are the police sure?'

With some pride in her voice, Julie continued, 'David's security people dug out the necessary information. Officially, only the police are authorized to confront a suspect, and it seems the police got involved again this afternoon. She bluffed for a while, but when they put on the pressure, she gave in and confessed. David said she admitted she still had the things. She's been carrying them around in her bag the whole time because she didn't know where to hide them.'

'How did they find out she was the culprit? It can't have been through fingerprints or suchlike. She works in that office, and has access to the cupboard where they kept the finds. She's Alex's assistant. Her fingerprints must be plastered all over the place.'

'That was one of the things that hindered police investigations. Apart from Alex and Gloria's fingerprints, there were no others on the cupboard. You were there, but Alex confirmed you didn't touch anything, so they didn't find any strange prints. They've now figured out that Gloria just helped herself to a couple of items.'

'But why? She is an intelligent, highly trained archaeologist. She's been on other excavations with Alex. I remember her telling me that she wanted to be with him on any of his future digs, too. She must have realized that if she got caught it would put an end to her professional career.'

'They are still questioning her. No doubt she'll eventually get round to saying why.'

'How did David's people get on to her?'

'They started shadowing any people they thought might be involved.'

'You mean Alex?'

'Yes. They had to watch all the people who had the chance to steal the finds.'

Kim spluttered, 'But that means they've been checking me too!'

'I knew you wouldn't like that, but they had to be perfectly fair. You had nothing to hide, so it doesn't really matter, does it?'

Kim was indignant. 'It does, actually.

I object to people spying on me. It has nothing to do with whether someone is guilty or not. I just don't like the idea.'

'They had to check everyone. There is no point in picking and choosing between possible suspects when investigating a crime. That would be giving preferential treatment to someone.'

'I understand why, but I don't have to approve. How did they find out Gloria did it, if there were no clues like fingerprints? What was her motive? She seemed completely absorbed in her work, and she admired Alex, anyone could see that.'

'They just put two and two together. In the beginning, they questioned her about the work she did. You'd be surprised how much people talk and give things away when they feel comfortable and safe. Then they listened in on her conversations when she was out with friends in the evenings. What they heard strengthened their belief that she was the culprit.'

Kim felt uncomfortable with the

thought that someone had been checking on her too. She hadn't noticed anything unusual. Julie's voice cut in on her thoughts again.

'Once they suspected Gloria, they started wondering how she intended to get rid of the things. She was too professional, too much of an archaeologist, to just throw them in the bin or in the river. That was her downfall. One of David's men stumbled across a coin up for sale on eBay. It matched the description and appearance of one of the coins from the site. They contacted the seller to ask for details of where it had been registered. Back came the answer that the source was unknown. Usually that's a sign that things are either fake or stolen. Apparently you should be able to trace genuine ancient artefacts back to where they were first registered. Anyway . . . David's people still said that they were very interested. Gloria took the bait. They arranged to meet personally. The bogus buyer used the excuse that he wanted to deal in cash, rather than the deal going via his bank account. They arranged to meet in a café in London, and when she walked in — bingo!'

'She must have been shocked.'

'Lost for words, and then she broke down in a torrent of tears. She'd have been untraceable if she'd thrown them away.'

Someone shouted to Julie in the background. 'Look, I've got to go. I promised to take part in a charity run. It starts in ten minutes.'

'But you haven't explained what her motive was!'

'Sorry! It will have to wait. I'll try to come home on the weekend. Perhaps I can persuade David to come with me, if he can get away. I hope that's okay with you? I'll let you know definitely later in the week.' She heard Kim's indrawn breath. 'Now, don't panic! David likes you, I've told him all about Uncle Jack, and he genuinely enjoys being with 'normal people in normal surroundings'. Don't get out the best china or polish the toilet! It's not necessary. I don't know if he can get rid of his watchdogs for the weekend, but I'll try to persuade him to. I'll tell you all the rest of the story about Gloria when we come over. Love to Uncle Jack and Linda. See you!'

Kim sat staring into empty air for a couple of seconds. Kim had tried to explain who David was to her uncle, and what he stood for. Uncle Jack was only interested in whether or not he was a decent bloke. She wondered how someone like David, with his hand-finished clothes and made-to-measure shoes, would fit into their world — their confined space and their run-of-the-mill food.

In the end, she gave in, and put David in the smallest room in the house. It wasn't much bigger than a cubbyhole, but it was the only one available. She carried some things that had been dumped there upstairs to the attic. No one was going to need the sewing machine, a battered old suitcase, or a set of neglected golf clubs over the weekend. The boxroom was next to Julie's on the one side of the cottage. Kim and Uncle Jack had their rooms on the other side. The cottage's single bathroom was mid-way between the two sides, and it faced the head of the stairs. She'd taken Julie's passing remarks to heart, and didn't move anything around or spend time frantically cleaning and polishing. He'd have to take them as he found them. If he really liked Julie, he shouldn't care if her relatives lived in a rented council house or a cramped flat in a high-rise building.

★   ★   ★

David drove down with Julie in his Aston Martin early on Saturday morning. Kim mused that it must certainly have set their neighbours' tongues wagging as it roared through the village main street and down the side road to their cottage. She was nervous.

Julie piled out of the car, and with her usual gusto threw herself into Uncle Jack's arms to give him a hearty kiss. Kim noticed the amused expression on David's face.

He came towards Uncle Jack and stuck out his hand. 'How do you do, Mr Goddard? Julie has told me all about you. Thanks for having me this weekend.'

Uncle Jack viewed him for a second, and apparently decided he was okay. He shook his hand. 'Come in! Come in! And the name's Jack. You know Kim already.'

David turned to her. 'Yes; we've already met once or twice. Hi Kim! Nice to see you again.' He gave Kim a lopsided smile and lifted their bags out of the back seat.

Looking at it, Uncle Jack remarked, 'Good car, that. The firm's been around for donkey's years. Beautiful sports cars. Even before the war they had great models. Ever heard of the Mark II?'

'Of course. There have never been

better sports cars on the market than Aston Martins — that's why I like them.'

David was alongside Uncle Jack now, who observed, 'The James Bond films gave them a much-needed publicity push. There was the — '

David hurried to add, 'The DBS!'

'And what is your model?'

'Vantage S coupe.'

Uncle Jack nodded. 'It is a company full of history and initiative.' The two men were soon deep in conversation about cars and their quality through the ages.

The two women followed them inside. Kim was surprised that Uncle Jack knew anything about cars. His own Jeep only got attention because Kim cleaned it, although he did insist on regular safety check-ups at the local garage.

Kim told Julie, 'I've put David in the guest room. Will you show him where to find everything? I'll put the kettle on for tea in ten minutes — in the kitchen.'

Julie nodded in approval and gave her a quick peck on the cheek. 'Thanks! You don't know how happy I am to have David here with me for the weekend. I've been dying for him to meet Uncle Jack and Linda. He has to see where I come from, and the people I love.'

Kim nodded and left them climbing the stairs. She hadn't overdone it with special food. She'd kept things simple, choosing dishes she could make in advance and leave in the fridge to be heated when necessary.

Alex and Julie went off for a walk after tea. She wanted to show him the village.

Uncle Jack watched them heading down the driveway. 'He seems a decent enough chap. She must like him a lot. I can't remember the last time she brought someone home, can you? You said that he's rich, but I don't think that matters to Julie. Underneath all that dizziness, she's sensible, and won't be influenced by that sort of thing.'

'I honestly think she likes him for

who he is. I like him, too. I just hope it isn't a short-lived thing. This time, Julie seems to like someone a lot. I hope she won't get hurt.'

He shrugged. 'Better for her to get hurt than stuck with the wrong person. I don't worry about you ending up with the wrong man. You're much too sensible.'

The weekend went well. Julie helped whenever she could. David was relaxed and seemed to enjoy it all. The way his eyes always followed Julie, and the way they seemed to be on the same wavelength, calmed Kim's fears. He did seem to be in love with her sister, and she with him.

On Saturday morning she was passing him on the stairs. He stopped and smiled.

'I want to reassure you. I do like Julie. I like her more than anyone I've ever met before. In fact, I love her. I don't want to hurt her ever. Julie mentioned that you told her to be careful. I understand that, but you don't need to worry. It is not my intention to ever leave her with a broken heart, or make her sad.'

She smiled at him. 'That's good! I'm happy if she's happy.'

He gave Kim a quick peck on her cheek and they viewed each other benevolently. Julie came clattering down the stairs, and Kim left them to it. They were on their way to visit Linda.

Julie stuck her arm through David's. 'Let's go! You'll have to be on your best behaviour. If she likes you, nothing else can stand in our way!'

Kim watched them go, and somehow she realized that they did belong together. They were a perfect pair.

She managed to get Julie to herself later that afternoon. The visit to Linda had been a success, and Julie and David were going to the local pub for a drink after supper that evening. They'd invited Kim and Uncle Jack, but both of them knew that they would rather be on their own, so they refused.

When the two men were watching a

sports programme, Kim took her aside. 'You promised to tell me what Gloria's motives were for stealing those things. I didn't want to mention it earlier, in case David preferred not to go into details until the police had finished their work.'

'Oh, he won't mind. I don't know how important this archaeological dig is to him, but he is very interested. I don't think he would have put his security people on to it if it wasn't.'

'And . . . ? Why did she do it?'

Julie grinned. 'She was jealous. She was jealous of you. She wanted to make it look like you stole the stuff. She didn't like the sudden interest Alex was showing in you, because she had her own plans for him.'

Kim was shocked. 'Me? She was jealous of me? There's nothing to be jealous of! I haven't been alone with Alex very often, and most of the time when we met it had something to do with work.'

'Ah! But the attraction must have been obvious to her. She eventually admitted to the police that she hoped you'd get blamed. She said she hoped it would drive you and Alex apart because he could never like anyone who tried to sabotage his work. She wanted to drive you out of his life.'

Kim was lost for words for a moment. 'How stupid of her. She had no reason to believe Alex liked me in that way.'

'Who knows what she suspected, what she heard?' Struck by another thought, Julie asked, 'By the way, what did Alex say when you explained why you left him and ran off?'

She managed to meet her sister's eyes. 'He didn't answer my email, but I wasn't surprised about that, because after I'd sent it, he was away for a couple of days. When he came back, he still didn't answer, and I decided he either hadn't had time to read it or didn't want to reply. I did get up enough courage to phone him: I left a message. Again, there was no reaction. I saw him in my office the other day, and from his behaviour I could tell he was embarrassed or annoyed. I followed his lead and pretended we were just working acquaintances. He did seem puzzled, but neither of us mentioned our walk. I assume he didn't want to refer to it again and was afraid I'd cause some kind of scene, so I kept quiet.'

'What do you mean, he didn't answer your email or phone call? Did you ask him if he'd received them?'

She was momentarily speechless. 'No, I just presumed he had. I didn't want to rub salt into his wounds, or mine. Why should I ask?'

'You sent the email to his office address?'

She nodded.

'And the telephone call? Did you speak to someone, or leave a message on the answering machine?'

'I left a message with Gloria, asking him to call me back.' Her voice faded slightly when she thought about the possibilities. Looking at her sister's expression, she said, 'You think . . . ?'

Julie nodded. 'You bet! She buried both of your messages six feet under, so that he'd never receive them! She'd stolen the finds, and wasn't sure how successful she'd be in getting you blamed for that. Your messages gave her another chance to put a spoke in the wheel. She hoped he'd never find out. She probably worked out from the wording that you two needed to sort out a snag verbally. She wanted to sabotage that. She was almost successful, wasn't she?'

Kim struggled to be sensible as Julie continued, 'What a bitch! She must have realized he wasn't interested in her. You said she'd been on other digs with him. If he'd been interested, they'd have been a pair sharing their private and professional lives by now. Some women just don't accept defeat!'

Feeling despondent, but attempting to hide it, Kim tried to sound lively. 'Well, it's too late for me now. I gave him the cold shoulder. He's not likely to coming running in my direction again: he's too proud to do that.'

Julie stuck her hands on her hips. 'He won't if you don't do something about it! You have to explain what happened. You need to tell him Gloria had her hands in the cooking pot.'

'What good will it do? He probably thinks I'm an idiotic fool.'

'If it was me, I'd fight for him. I'd want him to know what had happened, no matter what! I'd want him to know that I wasn't entirely responsible for the cool reception he received last time we met — even if he never wanted to see me again.'

After Julie and David left for a comfortable date in the local pub, Kim stared unseeingly at a thriller on the TV screen and thought about Julie's words. She was right. She didn't know where she'd find the courage, but she would try to explain what she thought had happened. She didn't want Alex to think badly of her.

David seemed to enjoy the weekend. He and Julie left after lunch on Sunday, and he said he hoped to see them again soon. Kim was reassured. Julie looked happy, and David had done all he could to fit in with them. He clearly adored Julie, and as they drove away, Kim prayed that it would turn out well for both of them. Even Uncle Jack had said he liked him, and that was an accolade he hadn't given many people.

11

On Monday, the office was agog with the news that Gloria was responsible for the artefact theft. Everyone knew her. She had always pointed out fervently to one and all how important she was on site, and to the project as a whole.

Even Mr Booth stopped for a few moments at Kim's desk to talk about it. He ran his hand over his sparse hair. 'It's incredible! What on earth was she thinking of? She's a highly qualified academic with an impressive reputation, and she's thrown it all away for the sake of a few artefacts. I think Alex noticed her when she was still one of his students at the university, because even in those days she was very clever and adaptable. She helped on several excavations after she had her degree. They were always remarkable digs, and they found a striking number of interesting and exciting things. I can't figure out why she went off the rails.'

Kim tapped the papers on her desk into a tidy block. 'I expect she regrets it, but it's too late now. I presume it means her archaeological career is at an end?'

'Most certainly! Even if she gets away with a probationary sentence, stealing is a civil offence. No one who checks her record will ever employ her again on anything to do with excavation work.' He shrugged his shoulders. 'She'll have to make do with teaching history, or being in charge of an archive.' He looked out of the window. 'I'm not even sure if she'd be allowed to do that. There's always the question of ethics and morals. She'll definitely have trouble finding any job where she'd need to handle actual finds. She has a master's degree, but no PhD, and she'll find it almost impossible to get one now. The word will get around.'

Kim nodded and wanted to change the subject. 'Do you mind if I finish an hour early this afternoon, Mr Booth?

I'll work through my lunch break to make up any lost time. I need to see someone.'

He waved his hand. 'Of course! That's okay by me. Most people don't even bother to ask. They just leave, and no one knows where they've gone. Sometimes it's quite annoying!'

Derek and the rest of the people in the department were shocked by the news. No one understood why she'd done it. Because of Julie's explanation, Kim knew jealousy had prevailed over Gloria's common sense. Gloria would probably declare it had been because she wanted extra money. She would never admit publicly to the real reason.

Kim was nervous when she set out to see Alex. She'd borrowed the Jeep again this morning because she'd made up her mind to talk to him and finally sort things out, no matter where it led.

The closer she drew to the excavation site, the more nervous she became. While still on the way, she even pulled into a side road for a moment. Parked in a gap leading to a field, she stared beyond the locked gate. At the far end of the field, a river was moving sluggishly along, past waterside willows with their boughs waving and weaving over the clear water. Some cows were wandering around, stopping contentedly now and then for another mouthful of lush grass.

Kim pulled herself together. Did she want to sit here watching cows until it was too late, or did she want to explain things to Alex, and perhaps win his good opinion again? She started the engine and reversed out, rejoining the main road and following the route to Gough's Burrow.

She parked among a cluster of remaining vehicles and noticed Alex's car was one of them. She got out and straightened her anorak. Shoving the keys into one of the pockets, she marched determinedly towards his office. She glanced across and noticed there were still people working on site.

They must have heard about Gloria too. She wondered what they thought.

Taking a deep breath, she knocked softly and heard him say, 'Come in!'

He was seated at the desk, facing away from the door. He was busy with some papers and didn't look up. 'Hang on, I'll just finish this.'

Kim did as she was told and waited. Her breath seemed to have solidified in her throat. She was glad of the respite as it gave her a few seconds to study him. His shirtsleeves were rolled up to his elbows, and his hair touched the collar and needed trimming. Even as he sat facing the other way, somehow you knew he was in charge.

He swivelled around. There was utter surprise in his expression. It wasn't what she had hoped for, but she understood his reaction. He got up and came closer. She noticed again the tantalizing male smell of him. It was clean and fresh and had nothing to do with expensive aftershave. His looks totally captured her attention, and she had to concentrate hard.

'Kim! What can I do for you? What brings you here? Have I messed up my reports or forgotten something important?'

She felt uncomfortable. 'No. It has nothing to do with work.'

His blue eyes darkened and he shoved his hands deep into the pockets of his rumpled chinos. She thought she saw hurt hiding in his blue eyes.

Her stomach knotted and she gave him a smile. She won no answering one.

His voice was grudging. 'Then I presume it is something else that must be very important. Carry on and explain; I'm all ears!'

Her voice was shakier than she would have liked, but she had to find the right words, and she tried to remain sensible. 'It's about that day we talked about the theft when we met at the Forest Walk, and about the way I dashed off and left you standing.'

The skin over his cheekbones tightened and his mouth stiffened, then he shrugged and continued to wait silently.

'I know now — in fact, I knew straight away — that I was being too touchy. I realize you weren't trying to accuse me of anything. I don't know why I reacted like that and dashed off like I did. It was childish. I didn't give you the chance to explain. I did try to get in touch later, but I think you never got my messages, did you?'

Disconcerted, his brows lifted, and he viewed her for a moment before he countered, 'Messages? What messages? I hope this isn't just a fabrication to appease my sense of right and wrong so that we can act normally with each other again?'

'No, it's not, although I do need to soothe my conscience.' Her colour heightened and she wrung her hands. 'I did send you an email, Alex. I sent it to this office. I even phoned you once here at the office because you didn't reply to the email. I left a message when I phoned, asking you to ring me back. You didn't, and I thought you just didn't want to know me anymore.'

'Hold it!' He held up his hand to silence her. He stared at her, baffled. 'You contacted me here? I never received any kind of message from you!'

'I realize that now. Julie and I were talking about the theft and Gloria's involvement. Julie put two and two together, and guessed that Gloria might have blocked my messages for a personal reason. I presumed that when you didn't reply, and after my stupid behaviour at the Forest Walk, that you'd decided to ignore me in future.' Her emotions were spinning out of control, but she wanted him to understand, to forgive and have a better opinion about her.

He took a step forward, pulled one hand out of his pocket, and she heard his unsteady breath. 'I still don't understand. Why on earth would Gloria do that? Thieving was acting completely out of character, but why would she hinder messages? I take it you've heard she was responsible for the theft? She isn't even here anymore. I had to fire her, of course.'

She almost floundered, but she had to tell him the truth. She hoped her words didn't sound too spiteful. 'I presume she was jealous of our friendship and she didn't want us to go on meeting. I think she stole those finds hoping the blame would fall on me for the same reason. Even if the police couldn't prove I did it, she hoped the suspicion would remain, and it would turn you against me. She probably deleted the email before you came back from your visit to your old excavation, and she just didn't mention that I'd phoned and wanted you to call me back. When you didn't reply, I thought you were signalling me to back off and leave you alone.'

His mouth clenched tighter. He walked forward, stopping in front of her. Kim could see the white lines at the corner of his eyes. Her heart turned over as his glance travelled over her face. Her whole being was filled with wanting. 'She was jealous? She did all this just to keep us apart?'

She nodded and swallowed a knot in her throat. The sudden flame in his eyes startled her, but it gave her hope in a way she hardly hoped for. 'Yes, I'm almost sure it's the reason, although she'll never admit it in court.'

He looked startled. 'Do you know I have been feeling sorry for her? We've been on several digs together. When they told me she was accused, I couldn't figure out why she would act so stupidly. I've known her a couple of years. After what you just told me, I couldn't care less if I never see her again. In fact, I'm bloody furious!' He looked it too; his eyes were stormy.

Kim bundled up her courage. 'Julie heard the details from David. He had the information from his private security people after he'd told them to solve the theft. In the end, they got Gloria to admit she was driven by jealousy. I decided I had to tell you and put things right between us. I don't like being at loggerheads with you.'

'You don't?' His mood was suddenly buoyant and he gave her an irresistibly devastating grin. Her heart sang with delight. Gathering her into his arms, he held her tight. 'Thank heaven that you came. I've been completely miserable since our meeting at Forest Walk. I'd never have connected what went wrong between us with Gloria. If that was the reason, I doubt whether she'll publicly say so, either. I understand if someone gives in to the temptation of pinching artefacts, but not if her motive was merely to drive us apart.'

He brushed a gentle kiss across her forehead, and then his lips moved and his mouth covered hers. She returned his kiss with reckless abandon.

They looked at each other in earnest, and he pushed a strand of hair behind her ear before he kissed her again. 'I could get used to this! I've dreamed of it for such a long time.'

'Have you really?' The warmth of his smile sent shivers down her spine. She was helpless and in love. She had a feeling of peace and coming home.

Cradling her in his arms, his eyes sparkled. 'From the day we met, I knew you were someone special. I can't explain why. It seems that fate does give us all at least one chance of finding love, real love. I've never wanted half-truths; that's not what I'm like. I decided a long time ago to leave it up to fate. If I met someone special, I'd be glad to share my life with them; if not, I had my profession and my friends. They would have to fill the gap. I'm thirty-four, and have never really been in love. I thought it would never happen, but it has. The chemistry between us was perfect, and I thought things were going right for me at last — until that day you walked away from me. I realized what I said sounded wrong, and was why you rushed off. I decided to sort it out, but I had to postpone my visit. It looks like Gloria stepped in in the meantime, and did as much damage as she could while I was away. After I came back, I came to your office hoping to talk things through, and you acted like you didn't want to know me anymore.'

They exchanged a knowing look. Kim touched the side of his face with her hand and he kissed the inside of her palm. 'We misunderstood each other because Gloria wanted us to. She almost succeeded, didn't she?'

He laughed softly. 'She didn't! We can make up for lost time now. I'm only hoping you love me like I love you.' He gave her no time to answer. His kiss and her response were the answer.

She managed to scramble a few sensible thoughts together. 'Alex, I'm not what you need.'

He viewed her with astonishment. 'Now, what does that mean? What do I need?'

'You're a professor. I'm an office worker in a part-time job!'

He threw back his head and laughed. 'Don't think you can escape a second time! I didn't think you were a snob. We haven't been together much, but that's going to change from today on, and you'll see we belong. You are beautiful, you're caring, you're dependable and honest, and I love you. What more will I ever need?'

'But . . . but!'

He covered her lips with his finger and then with his mouth.

Kim hastened to say, 'I have applied to start a university course, and I am starting to look for a permanent job.'

He burst out laughing. 'If that's what you want to do, it's okay by me, but I want you for what you are, not for what you plan to be. You are the one who should be scared. I'm an academic who takes his job too seriously sometimes.'

She shook her head. 'That's no problem. I live with one already! My uncle is married to his work. Do you know that, not long ago, Julie warned me not to get involved with an academic like him?'

He laughed and cradled her in his arms. 'Your uncle is okay. He is good at his job, and has managed to bring up two nieces while doing so. How is Julie, by the way?'

'In seventh heaven I think!' When he tilted his head to the side and lifted his brows, she explained. 'She and David are like turtle-doves. He spent last weekend with us, and I admit that I now think he does love my sister. They seem blissfully happy together.'

He said, 'See! I told you to let things take their course and let her make her own choices, didn't I?'

She nodded. He swung her around gently and set her back on her feet before he wrapped his arms around her once again. 'At last . . . from now on, we are going to see each other constantly.' He looked out the window. 'Well, as often as my work allows!'

She laughed. 'You are incorrigible, but I love you too much to challenge that. I wouldn't want you to pretend or change.'

He nodded. 'We'll find out all the good and the bad and I think we'll learn to love each other more. I'm not sure at the moment if it is possible to love you more, but I'm going to give it a try. Okay?'

Kim looked into his eyes and thought he had never looked so contented and happy. She could understand that because she felt just the same about him. She probably looked like the cat that had found a saucer of cream. She nodded, and saw their future written in his smile and the intense happiness she felt herself by just being with him.

She glowed with the knowledge that he loved her. 'Do you realize you are my happy ending?'

Murmuring into her hair, he said, 'Am I? That's fine by me, but I'm determined that now we've sorted out some of the hiccups, we're going to share a happy beginning and a happy-ever-after — and not before time, may I add!'

★　★　★

Six months later the two couples toasted each other with glasses full of bubbling champagne. It had been a quiet double wedding: David and Julie wanted it to avoid the avalanche of publicity for as long as they could, and Kim and Alex because that was the kind of couple they were. Just their families and closest friends had been invited. It had been a wonderful day, and the two couples were now parting to go their own way. David and Julie were off to his island in the Caribbean by private jet, and Kim and Alex were going to Rome by car on their honeymoon. He wanted to show her the famous Roman ruins and his favourite places in Tuscany — and, most important of all, he intended to show her just how much he loved her wherever they were.

Uncle Jack watched them leave the cottage for the airport after a round of farewell kisses. They were no longer his girls. They were now someone else's wives.

Linda touched his arm. 'Come inside, Jack. Let's have a cup of tea. They'll be back before you know it. They've chosen such nice men. I like them both. They are in good hands.'

He smiled at her. 'You're right. They are decent chaps. I'll miss seeing the girls so often, but they've both promised to come and visit me as much as they can. Kim even suggested that they thought it would be an idea for them to make their permanent home with me. Alex has no objections. The cottage isn't too far from the university when he has to lecture, and if he has to go off to outlandish places where she can't go with him, she'll be safe here. They'll want to modernize it a little, but it would save them the expense of setting up their own home, too. Kim seems to like her new job in that auction house, and she's making headway with her university course. It looks like Julie will never need to worry about money! Their parents would be so proud of the girls if they were alive to see them.'

Linda smiled. 'You've done a wonderful job, Jack — and I'm sure they are
looking down and can see them, don't
you?'